BIRTHDAY SUIT

LAUREN BLAKELY

ALSO BY LAUREN BLAKELY

Big Rock Series

Big Rock

Mister O

Well Hung

Full Package

Joy Ride

Hard Wood

One Love Series dual-POV Standalones

The Sexy One

The Only One

The Hot One

Sports Romance

Most Valuable Playboy

Most Likely to Score

Standalones

The Knocked Up Plan

Stud Finder

My Charming Rival

My Sexy Rival

The No Regrets Series

The Thrill of It

The Start of Us

Every Second With You

The Seductive Nights Series

First Night (Julia and Clay, prequel novella)

Night After Night (Julia and Clay, book one)

After This Night (Julia and Clay, book two)

One More Night (Julia and Clay, book three)

A Wildly Seductive Night (Julia and Clay novella, book 3.5)

The Joy Delivered Duet

Nights With Him (A standalone novel about Michelle and Jack)

Forbidden Nights (A standalone novel about Nate and Casey)

The Sinful Nights Series

Sweet Sinful Nights

Sinful Desire

Sinful Longing

Sinful Love

The Fighting Fire Series

Burn For Me (Smith and Jamie)

Melt for Him (Megan and Becker)

Consumed By You (Travis and Cara)

The Jewel Series

A two-book sexy contemporary romance series

The Sapphire Affair

The Sapphire Heist

This story is dedicated to Jeanne Blum and Elizabeth Mantia

PROLOGUE

Leo

Let's get one thing out of the way real fast. Regret is a waste of time. I don't believe in it—never have, never will. I try to live my life without that useless emotion.

You know those articles where the journalist asks old people what they would have done differently, and they list all sorts of stuff—be a better friend, call your mom, tell the woman you love her? You don't want to be that person.

There's a simple way to avoid it.

Do the good shit now.

Say yes to that crazy job offer, ask out the girl who's out of your league, climb the mountain and kiss the sky.

You'll thank yourself later.

But the flip side of that kind of life is this: you need

some rules. A few basic guidelines to follow to navigate the potholes.

Over the years I've assembled my top picks. Some from experience, some from listening to others.

Allow me to share my hard-won wisdom.

1. If you have to sniff the food in your fridge to decide if you can eat it, just toss it. You'll be glad you did tomorrow.

2. You can tell everything you need to know about a person by how he or she treats the waiter.

3. Turn down that last tequila shot. Trust me on this one.

4. If your woman sends you to the store to pick up something, get that something, not another version you think is better. Her version is *always* the right one.

5. You can't put your foot in your mouth if it's closed.

6. No dude ever gets in trouble while cleaning the kitchen.

7. Don't live to work; work to live.

8. If you tell the truth, you don't have to remember anything.

9. Don't get a tattoo that's longer than your dick.

10. Men should never wear black jeans.

That's my list and I'm sticking to it. Those mantras have served me well. They've made me the man I am today —successful, wise, and satisfied.

There's one more though. An addendum, if you will. The postscript you need to achieve a life well-lived. This ought to be so damn easy that no one makes this mistake.

Gather close.

Write it down.

Follow this one to the motherfucking letter.

No matter what, don't fall in love with your best friend's girl.

Too bad that ship sailed long ago for me.

1

LEO

Real men like chocolate. And they aren't afraid to show it.

I have no shame over my love for this substance. I love it when it's dark, when it's bitter, when it's semi-sweet. I love it slathered on ice cream; crafted into truffles, bars, and squares; or filled with nuts, fruit, or liqueur.

But there's one form I can't stand.

Chocolate fountains.

We're talking the hardest of hard limits, especially here at The Big Chocolate Show in the heart of Manhattan.

As I head down the aisle in hot pursuit of the next rising star, I'm transfixed by a guy in the booth a few feet ahead. He has a bushy beard and gnarly hands, and he swipes his index finger through the chocolate stream in front of him.

Then licks said finger.

He wipes the chocolate drops from his beard.

And proceeds to lick that off his fingers too.

Shuddering, I jerk my gaze away from the Finger-Licking Good booth. This is worse than going to see the latest Ed Helms F-bomb laden comedy and getting hit with a preview for a "snowman came to life and eviscerated me with an icicle" flick. I don't want horror trailers before my adult comedies, nor do I want to see cesspools of chocolate when I'm hunting for the next great chocolatier.

I adjust my cranberry-colored tie and turn into the Heavenly booth, admiring the classy layout, from the simple oak tables to the stone bowls the chocolates lounge in invitingly with silver tongs beside them.

Yes, tongs. Because chocolates should be distributed in public by tongs, not fingers.

With her usual cheery grin, our freckle-faced marketing director waves me over from her spot manning the table. Or *womanning* the table, as Ginny likes to say. She scans left, then right. Coast is clear. There's a lull in the booth action. She drops her voice to a clandestine whisper. "Leo, I pilfered some goodies for you."

"Ginny, you are brilliant and also quite nefarious."

"I take that as the highest compliment, especially since when I was a little girl growing up in Sydney, I had secret dreams to become a chocolate thief."

"Glad to see we're making all your dreams come true."

She slides a green ceramic plate at me then presses her finger to her lips, her heart-shaped necklace dangling perilously close to the table. "But I don't want anyone to see you tasting someone else's chocolate. It would make us look bad."

I shoot her a look. "It would make us look like we were on a mad hunt for the next rising star to partner with." As the exec in charge of business development, that's exactly my role at this show—finding that person.

She waves off my reply. "C'mon. Play along with me."

"Fine. Fine. Cover me, Ginny. I'm going in." I glance behind me, like I'm checking for sniper fire.

"You're all clear. Go for it. I've got you." With a sly backhand move, she wields the tongs—God bless her —and drops a small truffle into my palm. "This is your kind of chocolate."

"Do tell. What is my kind?" I take the chocolate, half-expecting her to say "bitter," since she knows me well enough.

But her reply surprises me.

"Spice."

I arch a brow. "Is that so?"

"Absolutely. You tell it like it is, just like a pepper."

Laughing, I ask, "Is that what a pepper does?"

"Of course. All good peppers give it to you straight."

"Then I will give this my true and honest appraisal, as if you'd given me Veritaserum."

"I love it when you talk Harry Potter."

"You *only* forced me to read them."

Her jaw drops. "There was no forcing. That was love. That was only love I forced on you."

"And several thousand pages of reading too."

"That you adored."

"I did," I concede, since wizard battles rock, then I

sniff the chocolate. It tickles my nose with a little hint of fire. I pop it in my mouth, the sharp, peppery taste tangoing over my tongue. "That's a helluva kick."

She pumps her fist. "I knew you were a spice. I have others for you to try too. But first, have you found our next rising star for our fabulous boss? She's damn eager since the first partnership went so well."

"No one who's wowed me enough with his or her artisanal creations. Who does this deliciousness belong to?"

"I'm not telling you yet. You need to taste the others first." She grabs another small square, placing it in my palm. "Try this one now. But smell it first."

"As if I'd do anything but sniff it." I draw a deep inhale, letting it fill my mind with . . . a most familiar scent.

Dark chocolate. A touch of vanilla. A little bit of coconut.

And like that, I'm thinking of *her*.

A woman who smelled like chocolate. I imagine she'd taste like chocolate too. I've wondered about her far too much for my own good.

As the memory of her scent floods my mind, I can see her face, her cheekbones, her mismatched eyes—one green, one blue. Or as she liked to say, one green, one *not so green*.

An impish smile.

She was bright, bold, and a little crazy in all the good ways.

She'd convince you to dance on the rooftop, climb the fence at Gramercy Park, and order the hottest dish on the menu even though you wouldn't taste anything for days afterward. You only live once, she'd say. And when it came to chocolate, her favorite assessment was, "It's so good it should be criminal." Then she'd add, "But thank God it's not."

"Is it so good it's criminal?"

At the sound of *that* voice, I snap to attention.

Am I hearing things? I spin around. Maybe I'm seeing a mirage.

Here she is now. The woman herself, in the flesh.

"Not that chocolate being illegal would ever stop you from eating it," I say, since you can't greet Lulu Diamond with a "Hello, how the hell are you?" or "It's been forever." Lulu must be greeted in medias res, and then you simply must keep up with her.

My eyes rake over her, drinking in the sight. She always looked like she'd ridden in astride a rainbow-colored unicorn while fireworks rained down on all of us.

Today is no different.

She's decked out in an orange dress with sapphire-blue heels, and her Sarah Jessica Parker curls are piled high in a bun. She used to tell us she was mistaken for the actress, circa the *Sex and The City* years.

She gestures to the chocolates. "Nothing would ever stop me from eating my favorite treats." Lulu glances at Ginny, meeting her eyes then pointing to me. "Also, you nailed it. Leo's totally a spice."

Ginny pats herself on the back. "Knew it."

"But he's also a coconut, don't you think?"

"Is that so?" Ginny jumps right into it, like she went to the Lulu school of How to Talk to Strangers.

"You heard our entire conversation?" I cut in.

"It was either listen in or cover your eyes with my hands and shout *boo!*" Lulu says.

"But that sounds exactly your style."

"You have me on that one." Lulu extends a hand to Ginny. "Lulu Diamond. I love your necklace, and you have the best hair."

Ginny pats her red locks, her smile blazing as Lulu does what Lulu does—makes you feel like the center of the fucking world.

"Ginny Perretti. And you're hired. For anything and everything."

Just like that, Lulu is making best friends with whomever she meets. The woman I've known since that fated day ten years ago flashes a grin at my friend and colleague. "Excellent. I'll be there tomorrow morning at nine a.m. on the dot."

As a group of chocolate connoisseurs heads into the Heavenly booth, Ginny trains her attention on them. Lulu looks at me then smiles again. It's the warmest grin I've ever seen, and with it, her boldness momentarily melts away. It's replaced by something else entirely—a sweetness, a tenderness. She has that in her, too, in spades. "How the hell are you?"

At last, we can greet each other like normal people as we drop the rat-a-tat banter.

"I'm . . ." My voice trails off as I consider all the ways to answer her. Busy? Focused? Alone? Ambitious? Determined? Kicking unholy ass? Lonely? Escaping from the world? "I'm all good."

"So glad to hear." She glances around, surveying the aisles of the show. "I didn't expect to see you here. It didn't occur to me. That's so dumb. Isn't that dumb? Of course you'd be here."

Laughing, I scratch my jaw. "I didn't expect you to be here either. Maybe that's dumb too."

"I thought you were still in . . . Where exactly were you for the last year or so?"

"South America. I thought you were in California."

She needed to get away from New York, far, far away, she'd told me the last time I saw her, nearly two years ago, through tears and mascara-stained cheeks.

"I'm here now. Now you see me." She gestures to her trim frame. She's a sexy carrot today.

"You look . . . great." That's the understatement of the century. She's always looked fantastic, but the happiness in her eyes has been restored. At least I hope it has.

For a moment, her smile slips off, and in that sliver of time, I can see all the ways the last decade didn't go how she expected.

How *any* of us expected.

I blink away the past, shucking off the pangs of regret. Fuck regret. I hold out my arms for a hug.

She moves in closer, and I tense for a moment. But as she embraces me in return, I don't feel what I used to feel.

I swear I don't.

Years of training has paid off.

Lulu Diamond, I am so over you.

2

LULU

If Leo were chocolate, I'd easily add up the ingredients that comprised him. With a touch of pepper and a dash of spice, he'd be a strong, full-bodied dark chocolate, bordering on bittersweet. You'd pair him with a rich red wine and enjoy him by the fireplace.

Fitting, I suppose, with that whole tall, dark, and brooding thing he works like a charm. It suits him, with his nearly black hair, a Henry Cavill–style swoop to it, and a jawline the actor with the most coveted jawline would surely covet. Leo's light skin is more tanned than the last time I saw him. The other side of the equator must have done that.

I shouldn't have been surprised to bump into him here. But still, I was when I spotted his familiar silhouette at the Heavenly booth. I didn't think he was back in the country.

In some ways, I've never been able to truly add up what makes Leo tick. He's been both an open book and a complete enigma. Except one thing has always held true—the man can rock a suit. I gesture to his Tom Ford ensemble, minus the jacket he's surely stowed behind the counter. "I can't believe you're in a suit at the chocolate show."

"Would it have been better if I'd worn my safari shorts?"

I press my palms together, loving that image. "Please tell me you own safari shorts."

"Of course. How else would I have ventured into the depths of South America to find the best cocoa beans?"

"Ever the explorer," I say, since that is Leo to a T—always checking things out, wanting to test, to try. "Was it just like *Romancing the Stone*?"

He laughs, a rich, deep sound that warms my heart. "Exactly like it. I trekked to the heart of the Amazon, zip-lining through the forest to uncover chocolate and develop co-ops."

I punch his arm, like an old friend, since that's what we are. Old friends tethered across the years by someone else. Someone who was the sun, and we were his moons.

Now, Leo and I are untethered, and I don't know how we'll orbit without our star.

"It's kind of mind-blowing to see you again." I press my fingertips to my skull and mime an explosion. "I haven't seen you since . . ." I gulp. It's still hard to say. I don't know when it'll stop being hard to say.

"Yeah. It's been a while." He exhales like he needs to take a breather too. "How was California?"

Maybe we've both moved on from all the stuff that went down. I know I had to. So I chose to, long ago. "San Francisco was great. Exactly what I needed. I worked with Christopher Elbow, sort of like an artist in residence."

"But a chocolatier in residence."

"Exactly. I built up my line there while you were in —where exactly did you go in South America?"

"Brazil, Chile, Argentina, Peru."

I can't help but smile. "You always wanted to see those countries."

He nods, drags a hand through his hair. "A dream come true, as they say. It was a great way to spend a year. *Mostly*."

I tuck that "*mostly*" away in my mind, knowing I'll come back to it later, knowing it means something he's not saying. "And now you're here in New York again?"

He points to the booth behind him. "I'm back in the corporate offices, working on new biz dev deals. What brings you to this coast? Are you just here for the show?"

I start to answer, but as the words take shape, I wonder why I haven't reached out to him sooner. Maybe because I needed a fresh start in the city, unattached from all the men in my past, and from all the ways they were attached.

That's not the only reason. Leo was a fixture in my life for so long, but now he's finally found someone to be a fixture in his. Amy, his fiancée, seems lovely, from the little he's told me. Of all the women I've seen try to win his heart over the years—and plenty have stepped up to the plate and taken a swing at that fastball—she's seemed best suited for it.

But that's hardly an answer to his question, and I owe him one. "I returned to Manhattan a month ago and found a place in Chelsea, all so I could relocate Lulu's here and open my second shop. I'm all moved in now, and the important items are even put away. The shoes, my chocolate-making tools, and my collection of antique cookbooks."

Whew. That was a mouthful of news I dropped on him.

"Wow. I can't believe you're in New York. It's like old times," he says.

But it's not really like old times. It's new times, so I focus on what's new—me forging ahead at last in my business. Now nothing, and no one, holds me back. "I opened my new shop in the Village."

He stares sharply at me, his eyes narrowing, the dark brown in them oddly icy. He heaves a sigh, shakes his head. "You're in so much trouble for not telling me."

I crack up, grateful for the tension relief. I poke him in the chest. I'm a toucher. It's my mom's fault. I was raised by a hugger. "It's not like you were exactly accessible in the last year. Every time I checked your Facebook page, you were posting pictures from Machu Picchu or Rio."

"Spying on me, Lulu?"

"I've always been curious."

"And what did you learn?"

I park my hands on my hips. "That you didn't post often enough for me to glean any clues."

"And trust me, it took all day to post now and then. The internet service was terrible."

"Poor Leo. Struggling without his first-world broadband."

"It would've been a struggle for you too. Waiting for

Etsy to load for your daily online shopping ritual would have killed you."

"Hey, I'm industrious. I'd have shopped locally."

"Good to know you'd have had a solution to a shopping dilemma."

"So what's your agenda here at the show? I don't suppose you're still sourcing cocoa."

He tips his head in the direction of the chocolate fountain. "Besides trying to figure out how many people dipped their heads under that and licked it? Like that person is doing right now?"

I jerk my head toward the fountain once more, and sure enough, it's a repeat of my friend's kid's birthday party when the guest of honor shotgunned chocolate.

Admittedly, I was tempted too.

If I had my own private chocolate fountain, I'd absolutely dart out my tongue into the stream every day. I'll be honest—I do love me some high-end chocolates, but every now and then, I like to slum it at a chocolate fountain.

Right now, an intrepid teenager in a skater T-shirt—likely on a dare from his buddies—is drinking a stream of chocolate. He's adjusting himself under the liquid, bumping the silver trough slightly.

"I feel like that might be a signal to skedaddle." I glance at my watch. "Plus, I have to do a demo in fifteen minutes on the center stage." And yet, I don't want this time with Leo to end. "But I'd love to catch up. Do you want to go to a hot chocolate tasting class later? There's one at three thirty. I hear this buttoned-up sommelier is running it. We could ask crazy questions and try to stump him. Even throw riddles at him. *I'm sometimes a bar, but I'm not made of metal. I'm sometimes a chip, but I'm not made of potato.*" I'm talking too fast. I'm nervous. Seeing Leo is stranger than I thought it would be.

Or rather, seeing him by myself is what's throwing me off.

"The answer is chocolate."

I stomp my foot dramatically.

"You gave me an easy one. Regardless, I would love to stump a chocolate sommelier and also hear what you've been up to," he says, as the guy in the skater shirt hoots victoriously, thrusts his arms in the air, and then takes off running, his buddies by his side. Yes, definitely a dare. We scoot closer to Finger-Licking Good to avoid being trampled. The fountain gurgles louder. "But first, what demo are you doing?"

I smile, proud of my news. "I was asked to appear at the James Carson booth."

His eyes widen, flickering with astonishment. "You won that award?"

"I did."

"Damn, Lulu. That's amazing." He reaches for me, to tug me in for another hug perhaps.

But it's not a hug that comes next.

Out of nowhere, a sharp pain radiates in my arm, and it takes a millisecond to register that someone has knocked into my shoulder blade, so I bump into the chocolate fountain. Leo yanks me away.

But my heel catches on the rug.

Then on something slippery.

And wet.

Heels are the devil, and my shoe snags as the world tilts and I lose my balance, the scuffle knocking me off-kilter. Everything goes belly-up as I careen, ass first, toward the floor.

But before I slam my back, my skull, and surely my tailbone too, Leo's right here like Superman, diving after me, grabbing me, and shielding me.

It all happens so fast, I can barely register the order of events.

The next thing I know, he's rolled me onto his chest, and I'm staring down at him. He's looking up at me, breathing hard.

Chocolate seeps into the side of my dress, since it appears the fountain spilled over.

But that's not what stands out most. What I notice above all is how firm Leo's chest is and how strong his arms feel, holding me.

I've never experienced an embrace quite like this.

Brown eyes have never looked at me so fiercely.

I swear, it's as if the armor he wears disappears for a split-second as he stares at me, swallowing sharply, a gust of breath crossing his lips.

Then, in an instant, the wild, foreign sensation is gone.

3

LEO

Positions I've dreamed of being in over the years? This would have ranked top of the list.

Wait. Not true. Only because I've pictured so damn many positions with her, how the hell can I possibly rank them all?

All fours is definitely up there.

Bent over the bed.

Reverse cowgirl.

But yeah. Fine. Lulu on top of me has to be near the peak.

And before other matters peak, I need distance. A lot of fucking distance.

Somehow, I disentangle from her at the speed of sound, lifting her up and off me as Ginny races over. "Are you okay? Or do I need to get you to the infirmary inside the Willy Wonka chocolate factory?"

Ginny's always ready with a Band-Aid or a joke.

Lulu cranes her neck to stare at the back of her

lovely orange dress that's not so lovely anymore. Even with my dive-and-grab roll, she still bore the brunt of the chocolate mess.

"I'll live," Lulu says to Ginny, deadpan.

"Do you want my shirt?" Ginny offers, plucking at her red pullover top.

"Only if you're interested in walking around in just your bra. And since I don't want to ask you to do that the first day we meet, I suspect I'll have to make do."

Ginny laughs. "But the second day would be okay?"

"Oh, definitely. We'll trade shirts tomorrow." Typical Lulu—roll with the punches.

I peer behind me. The back of my white dress shirt sports a tire track of chocolate. Meanwhile, a stocky dude who must be running the Finger-Licking Good joint marches over to us. "What in the ever-loving heck happened here? Did you jump into my fountain? Try to take a bath in it? Splash around and roll in the goodness like a pig in mud?"

I scoff, because he couldn't have it more wrong. "Are you kidding me? Your fountain bubbled over, and some kid had his face under the stream. That's what ruined your fountain. He must have bumped into it and that sent it spilling all over the floor."

His jaw drops. "Someone drank from the fountain?"

"Shocking, isn't it?"

The man scratches his jaw. "Come to think of it, that's not so shocking. It's kind of like a dream, isn't it? Chocolate flowing from a fountain. Drinking it straight from the source. What could be better?"

"Gee. I don't know. Maybe literally everything."

"Well, I'd say you should try it, but you clearly don't have a fun bone in your body. Now, where did this fountain-knocker-overer go, because I don't have time to mess around."

Lulu flails, pointing dramatically down an aisle. "He went that-a-way. Black skater shirt. Checkered Vans. You can probably still find him if you run fast enough."

"I gotta catch him. My boss will kill me if anything happens to the fountain, and if I'm home late, my wife will kill me." The Finger-Licking Good Guy mimes slicing his throat then makes a spooky, don't-mess-with-the-wife sound. With a brash nod, the square-shaped man takes off, running down the industrial-grade carpet, chasing a chocolate-drink stealer he likely won't catch.

I take a closer look at the woman I toppled to the floor with. "You look like you've taken a mud bath." I can't help it. I laugh. I laugh so fucking hard because she's absolutely coated in chocolate.

She laughs too. "We're quite a sight."

"We are indeed."

Her laughter ceases. Her brow furrows. "Shoot. I have my demo. How the hell am I going to do it looking like this?"

That sends me into action. My job isn't to stand around and let other people solve problems. "Stay here."

I dart into our booth, duck behind the stand, root around in a box, and find a chef's jacket and a hand towel. Ginny follows, and she's by my side, whispering, "The pepper chocolates?"

"Yeah?"

"They were hers."

I arch a brow as I grab a plastic bag. "No kidding?"

"Swear on my fourth grader."

I shoot her a most skeptical look.

She huffs. "Hey, I like my kid. But fine, I swear on my love of chocolate. Now do you believe me?"

"Indeed, I do. They were amazing. Did Lulu give them to you?"

"I snagged some from a booth. She wasn't even there. Do you know what this means?"

"What does it mean?"

"It means this was meant to be."

"If I were a conspiracy theorist, I'd say you planned this."

"But you're not a conspiracy theorist. You just believe in fate."

"Ha. I do not whatsoever believe in any such mumbo jumbo. If I believed in the poetic notion of some grand kismet scheme, I'd be in a whole different position than the one I'm in now."

The position I'm in now has nothing to do with fate, I remind myself privately.

Like I need the reminder.

But I repeat the mantra in my head anyway.

There is only choice or no choice.

My choice right now, amid the noise and clatter of this epic chocolate show fail, is singular—fix shit. Save the day for Lulu. Demos at The Big Chocolate Show are career-making. Lulu can't miss hers.

I rush out of the booth, rejoin Lulu, and hand her the towel. Quickly, she wipes down her arms. As I guide her through the crowds, I tell her she can wear the chef jacket for her demo.

She darts into the restroom and pops back out a minute later with clean hands and arms. She takes the chef jacket from me. "You saved the day." Her smile shines with the wattage of the sun.

"See how it fits first before you pronounce me king of awesome."

"I'll make it fit, and *then* pronounce you ruler of awesome."

I go into the men's room, wash up, and unbutton my shirt. The back is covered but my shirt is, fortunately, the only collateral damage. My pants are fine. I stuff the shirt inside the plastic bag and take a minute to breathe, checking out my reflection in the mirror. I'm wearing a white T-shirt. Not my most professional style but it'll do in a pinch. Good thing I haunt the gym regularly.

I take a moment to add up the facts, only the facts.

Lulu is here.

She's living in New York.

I'm living in New York.

I'm about to add in one more fact, but I can't in good conscience go there.

Besides, my heart is pounding too fast.

It's from the incident, I tell myself.

It's from the adrenaline rush.

It's not from feelings.

I don't feel a thing.

I leave the men's room, take a drink from the water fountain, and wipe my hand across my mouth.

When I look up, she's there.

With outstretched arms, she spins in a circle, waiting for an appraisal of her new outfit.

Her new, jaw-dropping, sexy-as-sin, might-as-well-throw-in-the-towel-and-raise-the-white-flag-of-surrender outfit.

What the hell was I thinking?

I clearly wasn't using my brain at all. Because she's even more alluring in this garb.

She's only wearing the chef jacket and heels.

"Are you . . .?" I gesture to the outfit, the end of my words making my meaning clear. *Are you naked under that?*

She rolls her eyes. "Please. I have on my alpaca panties."

"Alpaca panties?"

Her eyes twinkle. "I couldn't resist. There was a sale on cute animal print undies with faces, you know, right here." She gestures to her pelvis. "A six pack of giraffes, zebras, dolphins, and llamas too." She casts her eyes down. "Wait. I have on the llama ones. I always get them confused."

"Alpacas have shorter ears. Llama ears are banana length."

She snaps her fingers. "Yes. Exactly. I'm wearing the big-eared animal undies, so it's totally fine."

Great. Now I'm thinking of her in underwear. In fucking llama underwear. Precisely the visual I've assembled way too many times without help, thank you very much. Minus the llamas, of course.

She tugs at the hem of the jacket, revealing the bare flesh of her thigh.

"*Lulu.*" It comes out like a warning.

She laughs at me. "Relax. I'm tiny; this jacket is huge. It's like a short dress on me."

"A *very* short dress."

"I can handle a short dress. I've worn shorter."

"Shorter as in ass-cheek length, Lulu?"

Her eyebrows wiggle. Her eyes—green and not so green—sparkle. "Yes. I've worn ass-cheek length, Leo. But I'm still decent. And you're still my hero."

She leans closer, rises on tippy toes, and moves her lips close, closer, closest. She dusts those lips across my cheek, and it's like she's an arsonist.

In one swift move, I'm on fire.

She grabs the plastic bag from my hand, stuffs her ruined dress in it, and hands me back the bag.

When she swivels around and walks toward the demo stage, "decent" isn't exactly the word I'd use.

More like decadent.

The jacket hits the top of her thighs. Her legs are toned from kickboxing—and I know why she boxes, I know why she started, I know why she doesn't miss her kickboxing sessions with her girlfriends, and my heart squeezes from knowing this.

Llama panty–wearing Lulu makes it to the cooking stage at master food critic James Carson's booth, steps up, slides on a lapel mic, and smiles.

As if it's the most natural thing in the world to do a chocolate demo dressed like the sexiest chef in the world. Looking like the woman I fell in love with ten years ago.

Mad, crazy, unrequited love that required years to get over.

And seeing her now, commanding an enrapt audience, wearing a Heavenly jacket, having concocted a chili pepper chocolate truffle that made my taste buds sing the "Macarena," it hits me.

Lulu should be our next rising star.

4

LULU

Earlier today I was swimming in a sea of chocolate.

Now?

I'm shaking hands with the woman who runs Heavenly Chocolates. Kingsley goes by her last name only, like the badass businesswoman she is. She doesn't simply nab honors as a top female CEO or a top Asian-American female CEO—she's plain and simple a top CEO. She's become renowned for her market acumen, her fabulous holiday parties, and her tastemaker skills.

The company launched its Rising Star line last year to highlight, market, and distribute artisan chocolate alongside its bigger, mass-produced treats, and it was a huge hit. It never occurred to me I'd be in contention for a role as Rising Star chocolate-maker, much less chosen in one freaking day.

But Leo had marched her over to my demo, and when I finished, Kingsley stared at me over the top of her red glasses, asked for some chocolate, and then rolled her eyes in a sign of unmitigated pleasure. Seriously, those food-induced eye rolls are literally the best thing ever.

Now, Leo's gone, and Kingsley has offered me the coveted post as we chat behind the demo stage. She grabs my arm affectionately, her swath of silver bracelets jingle-jangling against each other. "Just the other day, I was in your shop, gorging myself on those new Earl Grey creations. They are sinful. Positively sinful. Look what you've done to my hips."

Kingsley gestures to her hips, and they're not tiny, but they aren't an ox's width or anything.

"You look lovely."

"And I wear Earl Grey chocolate so well."

I laugh. "You wear everything well."

She smooths a hand over her belly. "And sea salt, and caramel, and lavender, and raspberry, and strawberry, and so on. But no regrets, right?"

"As I like to say, I never put anything in my mouth that I'll regret later."

She chuckles, squeezing my arm tighter. "Aren't those some words to live by, sweetie." She clears her throat, her expression turning serious, her dark eyes staring intently at me through the glasses. "Now, listen. I want you to make something amazing for us. I want it to light up the night sky. I want it to be so good Aretha Franklin would sing a tune about it, may she rest in peace."

Nerves slam into me. She's asking for the moon, the sun, and the stars.

I've been shooting that high for years. Shooting and missing by miles. I need to be able to deliver the solar system to her, starting now. I give the nerves the heave-ho, raise my chin, and aim high. "Do you think Aretha might have sung about a milk chocolate ganache with peanut butter and toasted corn? Or truffles with pistachios and cherries? Perhaps even a buttery caramel with dark pecans?"

Her eyes widen, and she lets her tongue loll out of her mouth. "Oh, I believe she'd be hitting the highest notes."

I breathe a sigh of relief, chased by giddiness. Holy shit. This is a huge opportunity that could do wonders for my fledgling brand. "Thank you again. I'm truly thrilled."

"Also, this look you have going on?" She waves a long red fingernail at my ass-cheek-length jacket. "It's hot as hell. But maybe consider some pants next time."

My face flushes beet red. "There was a chocolate fountain incident."

She furrows her brow. "What?"

"Never mind."

Now isn't the time to talk about what went wrong. A few years ago, my life was upside down. I was a pastry chef working in someone else's struggling bakery in the East Village and fighting to find a few free hours to design and create my own chocolates. It wasn't enough time. My dreams were tabled indefinitely.

Now, thanks to Leo, my dreams—the ones I clutched to my chest even in the darkest of times—are racing to the stratosphere. I can't wait to tell my mom and my best friends and so many other people.

When Kingsley is done, I look around for Leo to thank him, but he's gone.

I head to my shop, roll up my sleeves, and get to work making recipes.

* * *

I feel the slightest bit intrusive when I send Leo a text later that night, asking if I can take him out for a drink to celebrate. I imagine he's at home, curled up with his fiancée on a dark leather couch, watching Netflix and chilling while ignoring his phone.

The image should make me happy.

I was rooting for that for so long, hoping he'd find someone who fulfilled his heart.

He doesn't reply right away, so I send a text to Cameron, my best friend and business partner at Lulu's Chocolates, the guy who is handling our expansion plans.

Lulu: We're partnering with Heavenly!

Cameron: So much goodness it's like great balls of fire!

Lulu: Not too shabby, right?

Cameron: That's the stinking definition of un-shabbi-ness. Wait? Heavenly's the company where the dude you've been friends with since culinary school works?

Lulu: Leo. Yes.

Cameron: Interesting . . .

Lulu: Why is it interesting?

Cameron: He was best friends with Tripp, right?

Lulu: Yes! You know that! Why is it interesting?

Cameron: You know exactly why it's interesting.

I'm about to reply when Leo's name pops onto the screen with a text telling me to meet him tomorrow at The Pub.

I picture him in his apartment near the park, the one with the green awning and the doorman who always called me Carrie Bradshaw.

I can see the elevator, and with sharp clarity, I remember all the times we took it, heading upstairs to a fifth-floor dinner party. Dinner, wine, dessert, Scrabble, Cards Against Humanity, riddle books.

Now, I imagine Leo is setting down his phone, turning it to silent, and giving all his focus to Amy for the rest of the night.

That's the way it should be, and I decide that image must make me happy.

5

LEO

As the Arctic Monkeys warble at their usual Mach speed from the speakers overhead and some guy in shorts kicks some white-and-black ball on a TV screen in a sport I will never like, my buddy Dean pours me a pale ale, chuckling the whole time.

"Wait. Tell me again the part where you had the brilliant idea to partner with the woman you've been in mad love with for a decade."

I shoot him the sharpest of sharp stares. "I'm not in love with her. That ship sailed long ago."

Dean nods solemnly. "Right, of course, mate. The ship sailed around the world. Is that where it went?"

"Precisely."

"Or was it more like around the world and right back in the harbor?"

I sigh. "That would be stupid. Do I look stupid?"

With intense brown eyes, as dark as his skin, Dean meets my gaze, parking his hands on the bar. "Do you want me to answer the question seriously?"

Thinking better of it, I wave him off. Dean *would* answer me seriously. "No. Don't answer. But I *have* moved on."

He nods again and stage-whispers as he slides the glass of beer to me. "I get it now. We're pretending for the cameras, right? They're here somewhere. And you want me to go along with this ruse."

"You do know there are a million bars in New York City, right? I could frequent any of them."

His lips quirk up in an evil grin. "And yet you always come back to mine. Admit it. You can't resist the call of The Pub. Nor can you resist the call of me." He pats the wood proudly.

"It's only because you have good beer."

He scoffs. "It's only because I am the most extraordinary bar owner on this side of the pond. Also, because I tell it like it is."

I lift the glass, tipping it in his direction. That is indeed Dean's strongest trait, but he's wrong on this count. "Look. I freely admit I had it bad for her when we met. I had it bad for her for a couple years. I've never denied that. But the reality is I *had* to get over her, and I did, thank you very much. I couldn't spend my fucking twenties mooning for someone else's girl. I've dated plenty of other women. I've been serious with plenty of other women. Hell, there's Amy too."

He wipes down the bar. "Yes, Amy. Great example."

"She *is* a good example."

"Fine. You got over Lulu. You found the occasional woman to throw dinner parties with." He pretends to wretch violently, reminding me why I never invite him to dinner parties. "And, evidently, you've swung your dick around and fa la la la la."

I flip him the bird. "That's not what I'm saying, and you know it."

"I thought you were saying all the ladies loved you? Is it your broody, growly charm that wins them over, or your dinner parties?"

"No, it's my *huge* . . . personality."

Laughing, he raises an imaginary glass to me. "Well done." His tone shifts to serious now. "Level with me. Are you prepared to work with her?"

"She's a contractor. We're not going to be in the same offices."

"You completely dodged the question."

"It'll be fine. We're friends. We've been through plenty. And plenty of people who have history work together."

Laughing, Dean slaps his palm on the bar. "That is the best understatement among all the understatements in contention for Understatement of the Century."

I grin, shrugging. "Who doesn't have history?"

"You two have so much history you could write a new textbook."

"Look, I'm in chocolate and she's in chocolate. It was inevitable we'd wind up working together in some capacity. I saw her at the show, and I *chose* to introduce her to Kingsley. It's that simple." I point to the bar. "It's a choice you're here, right? And not in London still?"

"Sure, it's a choice. Or it might be that I'm simply a stunning sex god and completely irresistible to hot, inked, bearded professional hockey defensemen."

"My point exactly. You made a choice to move to the States and follow your guy."

"Ahem, my husband. I'm no fool. I didn't move without a ring." He waggles his ring finger, showing off his platinum band.

"You made sure he wasn't getting the cow for free."

"Exactly. This cow has a fantastically high price tag and is so worth it." Then, he makes sure I'm looking him in the eyes. "I'm only pulling your leg. I know you two went through the mill together. You love each other like we love each other." He points from me to him, then furrows his brow. "Wait. Maybe not at the beginning, because try as you might, I just wasn't that into you."

I groan, dropping my forehead into my hand. "Why do I bother talking to you?"

Laughing, he slaps my shoulder from across the counter. "Listen, all I'm saying is, once upon a time, you were in love with her. You kicked the habit, you moved on, you got over her. Which is fantastic. Hell, you went on to get your sorry arse engaged. Good on you. Now all you have to do is keep it on the level as you work with her. It ought to be easy, right?" Dean looks at me with an intense earnestness that's his hallmark along with the cheeky bluntness.

"I can do that."

On that note, the woman in question breezes in and drops a kiss on Dean's cheek, then on mine, smelling like coconuts and a summer breeze that stirs up memories.

6

LEO

Ten Years Ago

"Coffee. I need coffee." I muttered it like a mantra at six thirty in the morning as I opened the door to the Audi Tripp's father gave him when he earned his bachelor's degree. It was a gift that served double duty—a present and a dig at his mom. "Why did anyone ever think waking up early was a good idea?"

As we peeled away from the curb in front of our apartment, Tripp glanced over, his quarterback-in-the-huddle energy too much for the hour. "You can do it, man. You did it in college."

I shot him a dubious look. "Hello? Have you met me? I famously took no classes before eleven a.m."

"Except for one. You powered your way through Business Strategy at nine. Remember that?"

I scratched my jaw. "Admittedly, that was my favorite class."

"Or maybe it was because you had my cheery, happy face to keep you going at that hour. Remember my daily wake-up dorm room knocks?"

"Yes. It was like a rooster cock-a-doodle-dooing in the morning."

He raised his chin skyward as he drove. "Cock-a-doodle-doo!"

"Stop. It was hard enough to take in college."

He laughed as we drove from Hoboken, where we'd opted to live after graduation, toward the Path station.

He reached behind to the back seat console. "Do I know you or do I know you? I popped out early to grab this." He produced a cup of coffee, the deli kind with the blue-and-white writing and a beautifully curling plume of steam coming from it.

"*Dude.*"

That was all I needed to say. He knew what I meant —*thank you so fucking much*. Gratitude flowed through me as I drank the life-sustaining beverage.

"All right, so you're finally going to master more than boiling an egg?" Tripp pulled into the parking lot at the Path station.

"Please. I refuse to master that. Hard-boiled eggs are the worst. But the more apropos question is this—will you ever learn how to balance a checkbook?"

Tripp cracked up. "Why do I need to? I can always lean on you for that side of the business."

When we reached campus a little later, he went his way to his culinary courses, on a fast track to become a chef, and I went mine, to a program that was mostly on the business side of food management, but with a few food classes too. The candy company I'd snagged an internship at during my senior year wanted me to learn the business from the ground up, and it was paying for my additional school, now that I'd graduated.

I grabbed a spot at one of the kitchen counters, and as I was sorting ingredients, I smelled coconut. I leaned in closer to the chocolate in the silver bowl. Was there coconut in it?

"It's so good it should be criminal."

That voice. Pure and sweet and confident.

I straightened and looked into one blue eye, one green eye. A straight nose. Bow-shaped lips with a hint of gloss. A green sweater the color of an emerald. Everything about her was bright. It energized me more than the coffee had.

"But no one should ever outlaw chocolate." I spoke quickly. Usually I was the thinker, waiting a beat or two before weighing in. This time, I jumped.

"Can you even imagine a world where chocolate was outlawed?" The woman with the wild mane of hair moved closer to me.

"That sounds like a dystopian hell."

"I hear if you're very bad in this lifetime, you're sent to an afterworld without chocolate."

I shuddered. "I'll be a very good boy, then."

She nudged her shoulder against mine, nodding at the ingredients. "What do you say we crush it here? I have big dreams."

"Big dreams are the best kind."

She smiled at me, her mismatched eyes holding my gaze in a way that made my breath catch. I wanted to say something else, something witty or clever. But I figured there would be time. Maybe over lunch. When the class ended, we left together, and I asked if she wanted to grab a bite to eat.

Once we sat down, Tripp strolled in. He scanned the tables to find me, and a flicker lit his eyes when he spotted Lulu. Like a spark—a spark that wouldn't fade.

He parked himself at our table with a dramatic huff. "Do you have any idea how hard it is to boil water?"

"How hard is it to boil water?" Lulu laughed, Laurel-and-Hardying with him right off the bat.

Tripp dragged a hand through his blond hair. "It's virtually impossible. You have to turn on the stove, then pour the water in the pot, and then put the pot back on the burner. It's too many steps. Who can keep track?"

"I think you're supposed to fill the pot first, then put it on the burner, then turn it on." She counted off on her fingers. "But I understand it might be hard to remember these in order. Did you want me to write it down?"

"Would you please? It's too complicated without a cheat sheet. I'll never make it."

She laughed again. "Do you need a private tutor?"

"I do. Please, please tell me you're a water-boiling expert?"

"I can teach a master class in it. I can also make toast without burning the bread."

He leaped up from the table, dropped down to one knee, and held out a hand, clasping hers in his. "You're a goddess."

I laughed, only to cover up what I was really feeling. *Left behind.*

Some things you just know.

I knew then that he'd win Lulu.

Tripp had an easy way about him. An effortless charm. He was sunshine and go-for-it mornings. I was nighttime and careful plans.

When he returned to the seat, he extended his hand toward Lulu. "Tripp Hudson. You have one green eye and one . . . not so green."

Her smile grew galaxies bigger, like someone had seen into her soul. She leaned closer to him, their body language instantly fluent. "Everyone says one is green and one is blue. But really, they're just different shades of green."

"Everyone else is wrong. We're right. One is a darker green than the other. And you wear contacts too."

She shook his hand. "I'm Lulu Diamond. I want to be a great chocolatier, and someday I'll get Lasik."

"How fortuitous. I want to be a great chef, and I'll pick you up from your eye surgery."

As if he'd just remembered I was there, he jerked his gaze to me. "And Leo? Leo Hennessy is going to fucking dominate. He'll be running your chocolate business and owning my restaurant. This man?" He pointed at me exaggeratedly. "He's got game when it comes to numbers and business and how shit runs. No one is better."

I just shrugged, smiling softly.

Maybe I should have said something else.

But it was clear that the brief chocolate-utopia moment from class was no more. And that Tripp had won a race neither one of them knew had started.

I took the back seat.

7

LULU

Present Day

Three-legged stools work well.

Better than four-legged ones. That's what my friend Cameron told me years ago when I had explained that yes, it was weird on the surface, but Leo, Tripp, and I got along like the Three Musketeers.

He reminds me again tonight as I bound up the subway steps, phone to my ear, chatting with him as I walk to The Pub after working in the shop all day.

"It has less constraints that would make the stool wobble."

"English, please."

"It's the theory of the three-legged stool. Its power. Its strength. Its stability. Ideal governments strive for a three-legged-stool model because the foundation is solid."

"You're such a brainiac." Cameron is a foodie by job and a philosopher by heart. "Why is it more solid?"

"Why do tripods have three legs instead of four?" He's like a professor practicing the Socratic method.

"Why? Tell me why?"

Laughing, he answers, "Because it's the ideal number for maximum stability, but not too many to make it wobble."

"So Leo, Tripp, and I were better as a threesome than we'd have been as a foursome? Is that why we worked well even when Leo wasn't involved with anyone?"

"That is indeed why."

"What about when he had girlfriends?" I pause, reflecting back on those times. Truth be told, I didn't see him as much then. "I guess we never hung out as much when he had girlfriends."

"Because you hated them all."

My eyebrows shoot into my hairline. "Take it back. I did not hate any of them."

"Fine. You simply didn't think any of them were good enough for him."

"They weren't! No one was good enough for him."

"I love that you're the self-appointed arbiter of who is good enough for Leo."

"I like Amy," I admit, picturing the smart brunette I met once. "She was intelligent and sweet, and she seemed like she really cared about him."

"And it hardly sounds like it pains you at all to admit that."

I lift my chin as I march down the block. "She's lovely, I'm sure."

"Be sure to let him know she's obtained the Lulu seal of approval."

But something gnaws at me as I think of Leo's woman, and it's not about approval. It's not even about *her*.

I wonder how Leo and I will be without *him*.

* * *

From the day I met Leo in the chocolate course, we were instant buddies. We had that repartee that reminded me of all my favorite sitcoms that my mom and I would watch, then analyze, then discuss. Only Mom could make commercial TV educational. Bless her heart.

Leo made me laugh, and then as we came to know each other, he made me think. He was patient, more introspective than Tripp. He was a quiet rainstorm at night, the kind that turned the air earthen and fresh the next morning.

Tripp was fire and lightning. He crackled and burned, a burst of bright, dangerous light across the sky.

The three of us clicked. I'd at last found my people. My mom and I had moved around so much when she went back to school, then for her master's, that I'd never settled anywhere. I'd been forced to adapt, to make new friends every few years since I was a little kid.

With Tripp and Leo, I felt like I'd finally discovered friends I could have for a long time.

That's what we were for a few months. A trio of buddies.

Until Tripp grabbed my arm after class one day, dragged a hand through his hair, and said, "I can't take it anymore. Go out with me. Go out with me tonight."

I said yes in a heartbeat.

On our first date, he took me to play boccie ball. As we played, he ordered a beer. Then another. He'd only had two by the end of the date, and that wasn't a lot by any stretch.

But hindsight is twenty-twenty, and looking back, I can see clearly what I couldn't see then—the first sign of a coming hurricane that I missed in the thunder and lightning of Tripp Hudson. Now, I try to be wiser, to use my peripheral vision more.

I turn the corner, looking up at the wooden sign written in proper English calligraphy. Even though I'm eager to see Leo, my chest squeezes and my pulse quickens. One of the legs in the three-legged stool is gone. I don't have a clue how Leo and I will work without that vital support.

After all, no one makes two-legged stools.

As I head inside The Pub, I tell myself to focus on our friendship, not on Tripp and not on Amy.

I can't think about how handsome Leo looks casually sitting at the bar, chatting with his friend. It would be wrong to think of him like that, especially since he's involved. But my heart beats faster with relief when I see she's not here.

It sighs ever-so-happily that he's solo.

Then a dash of guilt chases me.

I choose to ignore it, sliding into my everything-is-fabulous mode, dropping a kiss to Dean's cheek. "Hey, you handsome thing."

"Hello, you pretty creature."

Then I squeeze Leo's arm. "And hello to you, most amazing person."

"Oh, please."

I stare at him. "Seriously. You're incredible. This opportunity with Heavenly is huge. Thank you. I can't thank you enough. Drinks are on me."

"Please don't wear them. I'd hate for you to lose another dress." He gestures to my striped dress. Green, yellow, and light blue. "By the way, your orange dress is at the cleaners. She thinks she can make it brand-new again."

I throw my arms around him. "You are my hero a thousand times over now."

He tenses briefly then hugs me back. When I extract myself, I turn to Dean, tapping my chin, thinking of what to order. "What should I get? We need something fabulous to celebrate."

He narrows his chocolate-brown eyes. "I bet you want something pink and glittery."

I love that Dean gives me a hard time. It's part of our routine and has been since he and Leo became friends a couple years ago. "But pink and glittery drinks are so delish. Let's be honest. You can make fun of piña coladas and strawberry daiquiris, but everyone secretly loves them. Leo, don't you secretly love piña coladas?"

Leo shakes his head adamantly. "I despise them."

"You're only saying that to stay on Dean's good side. You love piña coladas."

Dean growls at me. "Lulu, if you say those words again, I'm literally going to have to ask you to leave."

"Piña colada, piña colada, piña colada."

He points to the door.

I pretend to be shocked. "You would throw a nice girl like me out on the street?"

He pretends to be annoyed. "You think you being a woman is going to stop me from throwing you out on the street?"

"No, I think me being a huge fan of your hot-ass husband would stop you. Did you see that slap shot the other night?"

Dean's eyes light up. "Did I see it? Or did I fucking reward him for it?"

I smile and offer a palm. "Man after my own heart."

Dean smacks back. "It wasn't his heart I was going for. It was his—"

"A beer for Lulu, please," Leo says.

"But it was just getting good," Dean says. "Lulu and I have so much to discuss about . . . *rewards*."

Leo rolls his eyes. "Shockingly, you can imagine that's a conversation I don't want to have."

I bump shoulders with Leo then speak to Dean. "Leo's no fun. I bet Amy thinks he's no fun either."

Dean coughs, sputtering, "Amy?"

Leo holds up one hand as a stop sign, nodding to Dean. "Thanks for the beers."

Dean plunks a beer down for me, depositing a pink umbrella on the edge of the glass. Leo grabs the drinks, and we head for a table in the corner.

The second we sit, I nearly spit out the question forming on my tongue.

I'm crazily curious.

I don't know if I can wait any longer.

I'm dying to know what's going on with Leo's fiancée, and my curiosity is a living, breathing thing.

As he raises a glass and toasts our new partnership, I blurt out the question. "How's Amy?"

She stares at me with wide and curious eyes, asking a question I should have known was coming. But even when you know something is coming, you're still not prepared for how it blindsides you.

I take a drink, thinking about why I feel weird answering her. Maybe because there was a part of me that liked being able to say to Lulu that I was getting married. Maybe some vestigial part liked the shield it provided.

She must take my silence to mean something else, since she fills it. "I'm not upset that Amy didn't want to invite me to the wedding. It's okay. I understand. I mean, I love weddings. I love all weddings. They make me cry. I always cry at weddings, no matter what. But you know that. I cried at mine. Of course I'd totally cry at yours too."

A sharp pain lashes me at the memory of her wedding, but as I've learned to do, I shove it away, stuff it into a corner, and ignore the fuck out of it. I rub my hand over the back of my neck, half tempted to play with her only because it'd be funny, and Lulu loves jokes.

But it would also be cruel, so I choose honesty. "We're not engaged anymore."

Her jaw hits the floor, cartoon cash register–style. "What?"

"She's not my fiancée anymore."

For a second, it looks like Lulu is rearranging her lips from a grin to a ruler, and I don't know why she'd do that. I must have imagined it.

"I'm sorry to hear that." She reaches for my hand and squeezes.

I will myself to feel nothing. I *do* feel nothing. "It's fine. There's no need to apologize. It's all for the best."

"Why didn't it work out? She's great. You two were perfect together."

"We were great together. She's thoughtful and kind. She remembers birthdays and anniversaries. She liked to restore old furniture with me. She's pretty, and I definitely loved her."

"But that wasn't enough? It doesn't sound like there's any animosity, so I'm guessing there was no cheating or dismemberment?"

I crack up at her Lulu-ism. "There was no dismemberment, nor disembowelment. Only disengagement."

She frowns. "Really?" She seems immeasurably saddened by this, like I've somehow committed a sin against love.

"Sometimes love isn't enough. Sometimes it can't bridge the distance and the miles." I take a drink, reflecting on my year in South America, away from my then-fiancée. "And sometimes absence doesn't make the heart grow fonder. In fact, shitty broadband service makes the heart grow weaker."

"Seriously? You broke up because of bad internet connections?"

"I wasn't in major cities. We couldn't keep in touch. I remember calling her one night, and the entire conversation was like a bad commercial. *Can you hear me? Can you hear me now? I can't hear you. I still can't hear you.* It wasn't really conducive to maintaining a relationship."

Lulu stares at me like I'm speaking in Morse code. "You split up because it was hard to make a phone call from South America?"

Apprehension crawls into my muscles. "Yes. And we didn't see each other often either."

She leans closer across the table, her eyes locked on mine. "But you loved her?"

I grit my teeth, breathe out through my nose. "Yes, Lulu, but it's not always poetic. It's not about love conquering all. Hell, you ought to know that better than anyone."

She looks away, swallowing hard, and instantly, I feel like a jerk. But I also don't want to explain all my choices to her. "I tried as hard as I could with Amy, and it wasn't working—case closed."

She pinches the bridge of her nose, sighing. "Sorry I pressed you on it."

And I feel like a total shit now. "I didn't mean to get angry."

She flaps her hand in front of her, exonerating me. "No, it's okay. Sometimes I get caught up in all the poetry-of-love nonsense. My God, I was all about that." She forces out a self-deprecating laugh.

I soften my voice. I can't ever stay annoyed with her. "You weren't all about poetry. You were practical too, Lulu. You tried hard always, especially at the end. Don't beat yourself up."

"You were always the practical one." She exhales as if she's sorting out her emotions. "I understand what you're saying. I just liked Amy, and I was happy for you. It seemed like you'd finally found your person."

Was Amy my person? I'd like to think, for some people, there's not one person, as in the one and only. I hope that's the case.

"Amy was great. And I don't mean to sound cold and calculating. I loved Amy. I didn't propose to her on a whim. I proposed to her because I wanted to be with her. But duty called, and that was what I did. Even if the relationship was collateral damage. I was too busy with work, and I was committed to making the deals I was assigned to make. I couldn't do both."

"She didn't want to wait?"

"I don't think either one of us did. Look, in the end I suppose we could have chosen to be patient and see what happened after a year. But she chose one thing, and I chose another."

"Do you regret it?"

I regret so many other things so much more. So many things I didn't say or do.

"No, I wanted to grow the company, and it was an amazing experience in South America. I'm fluent in Spanish now. So there's that."

She raises her glass, toasting again. "To fluency."

Soon enough the conversation shifts to safer topics, and we catch up on other things. I tell her I'm still living near Central Park, I've become obsessed with South American history thanks to my time there, and I've committed to learning the history and geography of a different country every month. I'm also still restoring old furniture I find at garage sales.

"Much to the chagrin of your neighbors?"

"Ah, but they are no longer chagrined. I have a little warehouse space that I use for restoring the pieces I find."

"Why do you do it?"

"It keeps me busy, and I don't think about deals when I'm working with my hands."

"It's your necessary break from work."

"Exactly."

She tells me about her mom, who's still teaching media and culture classes at the college level. After years of moving around to earn an advanced degree when Lulu was younger, then to chase various teaching jobs, her mother has finally settled right here in New York, and that makes Lulu very happy.

She tells me she's living in Chelsea, has joined a new women's kickboxing class with her friend Mariana, and plans to connect with a local rescue so she can foster small dogs again, like she did in California for the last year or so.

"I can do that now. Tripp was allergic." She says it with a mix of apology and promise.

I run a finger along the rim of my beer glass. "We can do this now too." I take a beat. "It's still weird though."

"It is," she says softly.

"I can't remember the last time we went to a bar."

"Or the last time we went to one and didn't have to worry. It's freeing, in a way."

"Yeah, it is." I hate admitting that, but it's also a massive relief.

But even though it's freeing, the flip side is that the knot of guilt that started to loosen is tightening again.

Because I'm here with her, and he's gone, and there's a part of me that's truly enjoying his absence right now.

I'm enjoying it so incredibly much.

9

LULU

A few weeks later

I've been concocting truffles with pistachios and cherries, been crafting buttery caramel with dark pecans.

I've flown to Miami for a quick meeting with my business partner.

I've been working like a madwoman in the shop.

Now I'm heading to the office, and it feels like the first day of school.

Nerves flutter up my throat as I turn in the mirror, FaceTiming a suit-wearing Cameron in his Miami hotel room, since he's on the road for a few weeks – Miami, Vegas, Chicago. I adjust my collar and tug at the waistband of my pants. "What do you think? Good first-day outfit?"

When I meet the team today at Heavenly, I want to make a great initial impression. My contract started three weeks ago, and since then I've been working on the recipes. While I won't be debuting them this morning, I'm eager to share some details of what I hope to make for the chocolate giant.

Cameron gives me a cheesy thumbs-up. "You have my vote."

I arch a brow. "Do I detect a note of sarcasm in your tone?"

"Me? Nah. Never."

Huffing, I stare at him. "Why are you being a hater?"

He rolls his steel-blue eyes. "Two reasons. One, you called *me* for fashion advice. I'm the guy who has reduced his wardrobe to minimalist business basics, and when I'm not wearing a suit, I think jeans are acceptable for everything. Also, I wear Crocs."

I wince. "I'm going to pretend you didn't say that."

"But you can't unsee them." He points his phone at his shoes, and garish, horrid green Crocs fill my screen.

I slam my palms over my eyes, my right hand pressing the phone to my face. "La la la la la." I yank the phone back in front of me, wagging a finger at him. "Next time I see you, I'm taking all your Crocs and donating them. Wait. No one wants them. They will need to be burned as an offering to the gods while you ask for forgiveness for ever having worn them."

He cackles. "They're comfortable. Also, when women dig me, I know it's for me and not for how I dress."

"That's for damn sure."

"Second, you want to know why I'm being a hater?"

"Yes, I do."

"Because . . . wait for it." He wields his imaginary

drumsticks and performs a drumroll, then gets up close and personal, shoving his face against the screen and shouting, "YOU'RE WEARING A PANTSUIT!"

I glance down at my outfit, royal blue with slim, tailored, high-cut cuffs that show off my heels. "But it's a trendy pantsuit."

"There is no such thing. I know nada about fashion, and even I know that. How do you even own one?"

"I borrowed it from Mariana," I mumble sheepishly, caught in the act of having stepped in sartorial mud.

"Well, un-borrow it. You are seriously getting me down. My mojo is at an all-time low. Seeing you in a pantsuit is like seeing a unicorn giving traffic tickets. That shit isn't right." He waves his hand dismissively at the screen. "Now, I'd say go burn that, but Mariana might need it to scare people when she's in court or doing depositions. So return to sender, and let us never speak of this again, unless it is to mock you for that day you went temporarily presidential-candidate on me."

Oddly enough, I breathe a little more easily thanks to his *dressing down*. Truth be told, this outfit isn't me. I've known it since I buttoned the slacks—hell, since I checked out my reflection and called Cameron for a second opinion. Still, I want today to go perfectly. I've lined up all my ducks in a row—I've staffed up at the shop to ensure my partnership with Heavenly gets off to a flying start. I want Kingsley to be proud of me, and I want to do right by Leo for recommending me, and I thought looking more corporate, less candy, was the way to go. "You're right. Let me find something else. I love you for being so . . . diplomatic."

"Yeah, that's me. I was so easygoing in my assessment of the worst outfit you've ever put on. Now go grab something dope, as the kids today say, and look like a boutique chocolatier, not like a politician. No one likes them, no matter which party, but everyone likes chocolatiers."

"Except Willy Wonka. He was kind of a perv."

"He is the poster child for pervs."

I say goodbye to my friend; rummage through my closet; rip off the suit that isn't me in any way, shape, or form; and slide into a cute purple dress with white polka dots, adding a chunky red belt.

I snap a selfie, send it to Cameron, and am rewarded with a return text full of clapping emojis.

Cameron: Lulu and the Purple Crayon!

Lulu: Is that good? Do I want to be Lulu and the Purple Crayon?

Cameron: We have reached the end of your allotted questions, thank you very much. You may now proceed to the corporate offices of Heavenly. Please send a report by the close of business. PS I am on my way to meet a mystery woman. Do you vote Crocs or no Crocs?

Lulu: NO CROCS! ALSO, I WANT ALL THE DETAILS!

Cameron: You will get them in due time.

I stretch my neck from side to side, take a breath, and send a wish that things go well with his mystery woman. Then I visualize my day unfolding perfectly. I'll meet the team, share some of my plans, pose for a few marketing pictures, and be on my merry way.

Lulu: I am Lulu and the Purple Crayon, and I am going to look so dope in photos in my purple polka-dot dress.

Cameron: I know how hard you've worked. Go kick ass. You deserve it.

But do I? Does anyone deserve anything? I've never bought into the life-is-fair or life-isn't-fair debate. I don't believe certain people deserve bad things and others deserve goodness.

As far as I can tell, life is about how we play the cards we're dealt.

Today, I've been dealt a pair of queens. The last few years, I was playing with a three of clubs high, at best, and bluffing my way through everything. Now, I have something worthwhile, and I'm going to treat it like the precious hand it is.

* * *

I'm thirty-two, but in some ways, I feel younger. Perhaps because my twenties feel like missing years. Back then, I was stretched thin and pulled in so many different directions and none of them were the direction of my dreams. I would work on recipes late at night, wait up for Tripp, then fall asleep at the kitchen table, worried and wondering what else I could do to help my husband. I'd rise at six in the morning, crick in my neck, cocoa bean on my face. Money was tight in those days, my focus was narrow, and my emotions were spent in one store and one store only—my marriage.

I was running on fumes, and there was nothing left in the tank to build a business. Now that I've worked through the pain and the heartache, I'm a dog chasing a Frisbee with my career. I won't lose sight of it or let it go.

And as I look into the lobby mirror at Lulu and the Purple Crayon, I feel like a new woman with a new chance.

I head to the food labs inside the corporate offices of Heavenly and work with my colleagues there on the recipes I'm mapping out.

Later that morning, Leo texts that he's at a business meeting, but he recommends the edamame salad for lunch and he'll see me before the meeting starts.

I reply: Edamame rocks, and so do you.

As I send it, I smile, loving that he's looking out for me in his way. I lose a little more of the first-day-of-school jitters, knowing I have someone in my corner backing me.

At lunchtime I pop into the company cafeteria, where Ginny waves, motioning for me to join her. I wave back, indicating I will, then walk past a pack of guys discussing a call in last night's Yankees game.

One of them looks my way, then flashes a friendly smile. "Am I right or am I right?"

I doubt the shouter needs my affirmation that he's right, but I shoot him the thumbs-up, giving it to him anyway. "Totes. That was one hundred percent infield fly rule."

He jerks his gaze sharply at me, his hazel eyes widening in admiration as I head in the direction of the edamame.

Thirty seconds later, the shouter strolls over to the salad bar. He's tall and toned, and he sports a neatly trimmed goatee, the same chestnut shade as his hair. "Hey, you're new, right?"

I smile, eager to make friends here. "Yes. I'm Lulu."

"And you're like a play-by-play analyst. Whipping out that infield fly rule." He snaps his fingers with gusto. "Damn. Can I call you SportsCenter? Wait. No way. I'm calling you the Color Girl, like the color commentator. Scratch that. You're the umpire. I'm Noah Rivera. Want to join my fantasy baseball league, *Umpire*?"

Holy crap. He's already bestowing nicknames and asking me to do corporate-y stuff. "I'm not that good with fantasy leagues, but I can— "

"It's just something we do for fun. You should do it. You should absolutely do it. It's awesome. In our league, we go head to head with the guys and gals from Frodo's Snacks, Wine O'Clock, and Violet's Dry Soda," he says, mentioning a big packaged goods company, a vino distributor, and one of those hip, trendy soda companies. "The league is literally the definition of awesome."

He's the Energizer Bunny dipped into a vat of espresso, then pumped up from a session at the gym. "Sure. I can give it a shot."

"Email me. I'll hook you up. I promise it'll be rad." He shifts gears lickety-split, nodding at the chicken spinach salad on my side of the salad bar. "I'm training for a 10K. I intend to finish in first place, and my times are awesome. You know what that means?"

"You're going for a run the second you finish your salad?"

"After work, you bet I am. But right now? I need a helluva lot more protein with my greens. Do me a solid and toss me some of that chicken salad, will ya?"

"Sure." I deposit some greens on his tray.

He lifts his eyebrows like I'm the stingiest bastard in Salad Land. "A little more? I'm a growing boy, and I burn a lot of calories."

"Of course. Here you go." I serve him a heaping dose of salad, amused by his one speed—sixty miles an hour.

Then he surprises me, dropping his voice. "Put in a good word for me with the Gin-meister, will you?"

He's such a guy, angling for a girl through her . . . friend? I guess I'm Ginny's friend. "Should I tell her you're excellent at burning calories?" Then my eyes widen. "Wait, not that."

He laughs. "Tell her I'm supremely friendly."

"You're definitely extraordinarily friendly."

"So are you. Great to meet you, Umpire Lulu. Catch you later," he shouts as he speeds across the cafeteria to join his fellow Yankees fans. That right there is why energy drinks should be banned. That man likely has a secret stash in his cubicle and mainlines them in between spreadsheets.

I find Ginny again. With a neat red ponytail cinched high on her head, she points to the empty seat across from her at the end of a table. Like she's a taste tester, she has food spread out before her—a plate of carrots, a bowl of blueberries, and a tray with three different salads in the divider sections.

"Hey there." I sit, plucking at the strap of my dress. "It might be tough to trade shirts today. I'm afraid it'd be rather difficult for me. But I'd consider it for that necklace."

She eyes the heart-shaped necklace that dangles against her chest. "Difficult, schmifficult. I want a purple polka-dot dress. It's totally a fair trade." Then she smiles. "I'm glad Kingsley nabbed you. I was hoping it'd be you for the Rising Star line. I have to admit, I had an awful premonition it was going to be a male chocolatier again. Too many of the *stars* in the food field are men. We need more chicks. More girl power."

I take a bite of my salad, nodding. "I'm all for that."

She plucks a blueberry and pops it in her mouth. "But that's not to say you're only valuable for your ovaries."

"Why, thank you. Though I honestly don't know the value of them."

Ginny cups the side of her mouth and whispers, "I know the value of mine. They work too well. I have a ten-year-old. No dad."

I raise a hand. "I was raised with no dad. I think I turned out okay."

A whooshing sound passes my head, and I crane my neck as a paper airplane soars past me and lands next to Ginny.

She rolls her eyes. "Noah."

"Is he the paper airplane maker?"

She picks up the winged object. "He likes to send these to me at lunch. He's such a goofball."

My curiosity is piqued. "Regularly?"

"Once or twice a week."

"Pretty sure that means he's into you."

She laughs, dismissing the idea with a fervent wave. "Oh, no. He's just . . . festive."

I glance behind me, and Noah waves from his table. To Ginny. "No. He has a thing for you. A big thing. What about you? Is it mutual?"

"I'm thirty-five. I'm ten years older than he is. Is that terrible? Does that make me a cougar?"

"Perhaps it makes you wiser."

"But is dating him wise? My daughter's in fourth grade. He's only fifteen years older than my daughter. *Fifteen*."

"But he's not her father."

"I know, but still. Robbing the cradle much?"

"I don't think you should worry about that."

"What should I worry about?"

As I take a bite of edamame, I consider her question. I consider my track record. I consider what I knew and didn't know then offer my best answer. "Whether he's as good at dating as he is at piloting paper airplanes."

"Good point. But I'm finding it a bit hard to make that decision." She gestures to the vast array of items in front of her. "I couldn't even decide what to have for lunch."

"Dating and lunch are different beasts. For now, I guess you have a little of everything."

"Now that's an excellent decision." She drops her voice to a knowing whisper. "With lunch and men."

* * *

As promised, Leo waits for me outside the conference room, his back to me.

Out of nowhere, a wave of goose bumps rushes over my skin when I see him.

Now that—that's the kind of man suits are made for. Screw politicians. Suits are for men like Leo—broad shoulders, strong thighs, toned arms.

And he possesses another attribute that sure makes a suit look like it's whistling a happy tune being worn by him.

His *ass*.

Those tailored charcoal pants seem to hug his ass worshipfully, praying at the altar of perfect cheeks.

Tingles sweep down my chest, and absently, I lick my lips.

Wait.

I stop in my tracks, talking back to my wildly inappropriate self.

Did I just think of Leo's ass?

Oh hell, I did, says *Wildly Inappropriate Lulu*.

I did just think of his firm, succulent butt that's begging to be grabbed, held on to, woman-handled.

Stop!

I clench my fists, my nails digging in, a mildly painful bid to wrest control of the runaway train of my libido. I shove away the errant dirty thoughts. I should not be thinking about Leo's butt.

But how did I never notice he had such a fine ass before? I'm not even an ass woman. I'm an eyes woman.

When he turns around, his smile spreads lazily, taking its time. His grin is crooked and kind at the same time, reaching all the way to his eyes, his brown irises so damn soulful they seem to see inside me.

That's when I do a clean sweep of my brain.

I can't let him see inside me. He can't know I was thinking of his . . . *assets*. I'm here to work, not to perv on the man. After all, I'm no female Willy Wonka.

But, more importantly, I'm working with him. And yeah, sure, no one has asked me to sign a contract forbidding contractors like me from fraternizing with key employees like him. But hello? I'm here to work, and I need to focus on this opportunity to build my business at last. And to build it free of distractions of the male variety.

I vow to think friendly thoughts.

I say hi, then head into the conference room with him by my side. Once we sit down, I don't make eye contact. Not with his eyes, nor his ass.

Well, he is parked on it. It would be hard to check out his chiseled butt right now anyway.

10

LEO

I grew up as the oldest of three brothers in a middle-class family outside Philadelphia. My father worked as a manager at a hardware store, my mother as a florist. Our lives were simple. My parents worked hard and long.

When times were leaner, I tried my best to make sure my younger brothers had everything they needed —the warmer jackets, the better sneakers. At five years older than my middle brother and seven more than the youngest, I was keenly aware I'd make it out of the house before they did, so I did my part to put them first and to make sure I could contribute to the family too.

In high school, I snagged a busboy job at a swank surf-and-turf restaurant. Its sprawling oak booths and burgundy leather seats were home to the wheelers and dealers in the city.

I worked my way up from busboy to waiter, and along the way, I was privy to bits and pieces of the deal-making that went down in those booths. There, as I served porterhouse and Cobb salad, I learned the lingo.

Now, at age thirty-two, I have the job I want. I'm the guy who strikes the deals. I'm exactly where I want to be in business, and that's because I set a goal when I was younger, and I worked my ass off to reach it. When I went to college, I paid for it myself, thanks to loans and scholarships I earned.

I take pride in what I do, especially because I don't merely love deal-making—I love doing it for Heavenly. My family had one indulgence growing up—*chocolate*—even when money was tight. My mom would bring out a treat from her secret hiding place when we had all done our homework and chores.

As I grew older, my love affair with chocolate stayed strong. Work feels a lot less like work and more like an indulgence.

Now, the chance to introduce my old friend to my company gives me a healthy injection of pride.

Friend, I remind myself.

Lulu has only ever been a friend.

That's the truth, the whole truth, and nothing but the truth.

No one needs to know I once had a Pandora's box full of feelings for the woman.

Kingsley leads the meeting, and after a few minor items, she gives me the floor. "And Leo has found our next Rising Star. Leo, why don't you introduce Lulu to the department heads?"

I stand, gesture to the woman in purple and white, and dive into it. "I consider myself lucky for a lot of reasons. But first and foremost, it would have to be because, back in the day, I was this woman's guinea pig."

Lulu laughs softly, her smile warming me up. I swear I can see the memories flickering before her eyes —of late nights sampling goodies, testing recipes, asking me to try just another bite. Those were the nights I fell in love with her.

I blink the images away, doing my best to stay rooted in the moment.

"What a trooper I was back then. So gallantly offering myself up whenever she needed someone to taste test a peanut butter truffle, or a chocolate-covered salted caramel. Mind you, this was before salted caramel became a thing."

Lulu's expression turns faux-confused. "There was a time before salted caramel? Sounds terrible."

"The world before the salted-caramel craze was a devastating one," I say.

Noah chuckles loudly. "So, Lulu was one of the movement's founders, and you were the salted-caramel taste tester. That must have been so rough."

"It was difficult and incredibly challenging. I had to add in extra daily workouts to maintain my figure."

That's Kingsley's cue to jump in once more. "Maybe you ought to send me the name of your personal trainer, then. Because I haven't cracked the salted-caramel resistance code either."

I smile then cut to the chase. "Folks, Lulu Diamond has been crafting the most delicious chocolate since I first had the pleasure of tasting her creations. We're talking melt on your tongue, make your taste buds sing, and turn your world upside down with pleasure. In a word—*heavenly*. I am pleased she's joining us as a chocolatier in residence for the next year. Thank you, Lulu. It is an honor."

Lulu beams, and it's the kind of smile that can't be contained. For one terribly selfish moment, all I can think is *I did that*. A voice in the back of my head taunts me. *You're the one who can do that for her now in other ways. You don't have any competition.*

I cringe inside, telling that voice to shut the hell up.

There was never any competition with my best friend. I didn't fight for her affection. I didn't throw down the gauntlet and say, *My name is Leo Hennessy, and I am here to battle you for the green- and blue-eyed beauty*. We were all friends, and I never made a play for her.

He did.

I focus on the here and now, as Lulu stands. Her eyes shine with a hint of wetness. Lulu had the softest heart, and she'd cry at any sad story in the news or touching moment in the movies. She's tough as nails too, so I know she won't break down here. Still, I love knowing that my introduction matters to her.

She smooths a hand over her clothes, something I've learned is her nervous tell. But when she speaks, there's only confidence in her tone. "It's truly an honor to partner with Heavenly, and my goal here is quite simple: I hope to make all the customers as addicted to my chocolates as Leo and Kingsley are."

Lulu and I sit, and Kingsley takes the floor again, tucking an errant strand of silky black hair behind her ear. "Thank you, Lulu and Leo. And I imagine, like me, you all want this new partnership to succeed?" She looks to the crew.

Everyone nods.

"Good." She takes a breath. "But how badly do you want it to succeed?"

"So badly!" Noah shouts.

"That's what I thought. And while the last Rising Star did very well, we can't rest on our laurels. Finger-Licking Good has had a whole heap of press lately after they played the sympathy card when someone contaminated their fountain at the chocolate fair."

"Oh no they didn't!" Noah says, dramatically.

"Oh yes they did. But something's rotten in the state of candy."

"Please say it's not my favorite flavor of Mars bar. Please say it's not rotten," Noah mutters in a prayer to the gods of candy.

Kingsley whips her gaze to him. "You better not be eating Mars bars while I pay your salary."

He scoffs. "No way. Just testing you. I only eat Heavenly chocolate." Under his breath, he adds, "I only eat protein bars."

"Chocolate is good for you, Noah Rivera." Kingsley strides to the head of the conference table, taps the keyboard on her laptop, and points to the image projected on the whiteboard. "This is the problem, folks. Big problem."

An Instagram post from Frodo's. It's an array of potato chips, artfully arranged on a silver plate, in the outline of a lovely woman. Chip legs are crossed invitingly, a hand is parked on a chip hip, and the salty breasts are full.

Holy potatoes. Some chip sculptor turned salt and vinegar chips into something succulently suggestive. It's pure snack porn, and my mouth is watering.

Noah lets his tongue loll out. "Hot damn. I want to—"

Kingsley holds up a hand and slices off the dirty thought that was surely about to make landfall. "Don't go there, Rivera. Whatever you were going to say is, I'm sure, inappropriate for mixed company and for my company."

"But Mrs. Potato looks so hot."

Kingsley stares down the bridge of her nose at him. "I know. Trust me, I know. But that's not the big issue."

"Well, they are quite big," Ginny mutters, then gestures to the chip lady's knockers.

"That's what she said." And that's courtesy of Noah, naturally.

"The big issue is what Frodo's posted next." Ginny shifts to a more serious tone.

Kingsley glances at the offending photo again. "Thank you for bringing this to my attention, Ginny. Because this is a big, stinking, hairy hairball of a problem."

She clicks to the next image, and it's a caption. *Devour chips, not chocolate. Savory is better than sweet.*

A collective gasp echoes across the conference room.

Noah slams a fist on the table. "Those are fighting words."

"Plus, look at the comments. The likes. Dear God, the likes." Kingsley emits a long, tortured moan, like she's Edward Munch's *The Scream* and the complete and utter devastation of humanity has set in. She snaps her gaze away as if she can't bear to look at the number. "But there's more. It's worse."

Kingsley taps the screen one more time, displaying what I can only presume will be the pièce de résistance.

A Twitter post of a chocolate fountain spilling over at the chocolate show. And the words below it? *Potato chips don't make this kind of mess. Just sayin'.*

She slams the laptop closed. "And the Twitterinos love it."

Ginny scrunches her brow. "I don't think Twitterinos is a thing."

Kingsley waves a hand, four rings sparkling brightly as they catch the afternoon sun. "Twitteristas, Twitterati, Twitter-schmitter. Whatever. The point is, Frodo's is eating our lunch. And laughing at us. And do you all know who runs Frodo's?"

"Your sister runs Frodo's," Ginny answers.

"My older sister, Scarlett, who loves to needle me. So I did the only thing I could do."

"Challenged her to a duel?" Noah asks.

"Poked her till she begged you to stop? That's what I used to do to my little sister. My daughter tries it with me now, but I always beat her. I'm a champion poker," Ginny suggests.

"That's a good one, and I'll consider it, along with photoshopping a vampire bat on her face and posting that on her LinkedIn profile."

I fold my arms, groaning silently. Something's coming. I don't know what, but Kingsley can't resist a crazy battle royale with her sister.

One year, she and Scarlett hosted a competitive

costume party. The next year, it was a trivia matchup with prizes like movie vouchers and dinners at fancy restaurants, nights on the town and tickets to Broadway shows dangled in front of us.

Lulu looks to me with big, expectant eyes, asking silently, *What is it?*

"Wait for it," I whisper.

Kingsley takes a deep breath. "This will be good for us. It'll be a morale boost. It'll strengthen our teams. It'll bond us. It'll help us roll out the most amazing line of craft chocolate. Better than last year. Better than we've ever been before. Let's not forget, last year the Rising Star line outsold chips at many of our competitors. And I believe we can bring that same spirit to our rollout this year. Because this year . . ." She stops, sweeps her arms out wide like she's about to launch us into the *Hunger Games*, and let's hope she's not sending us as tributes into the wilds of Manhattan.

I wait, poised on the edge of my seat.

Just because I let Tripp take the lead doesn't mean I'm not competitive.

Just because I put my brothers first doesn't mean I don't care about winning.

I'm where I am today because I'm willing to go for it. Whatever Kingsley has for us, I'll rise to the occasion. Hell, for the costume contest, Ginny and I competed in the Best Pun category and won as "Green with Envy." She dressed head to toe in emerald, and I showed up as the letters *N* and *V* from Scrabble.

"This year, we are going to take on Frodo's in a multi-day scavenger hunt. And I bet the Frodo's CEO that we'd win."

Lulu's jaw drops, and she mouths, *Is she for real?*

I whisper, "We've done a few of these in the past. But don't worry. It's just for employees."

Kingsley clears her throat once more. "And this year, since our focus is on teamwork, bonding, and introducing our brand-new partnership with a premiere craft chocolatier, it would be a great honor if Lulu would join us on a multi-day, team-building, bonding extravaganza starting next Wednesday morning."

My spine straightens.

Shit. She's going to feel obligated. She's going to say yes. I should let her know I can help her get out of it if she wants. She's only a contractor, after all.

But Lulu nods excitedly. "I was hoping you'd ask. I love riddles, and I killed it at hide-and-seek as a kid. I'd love to do a scavenger hunt."

When the meeting ends and Kingsley's photographer snaps a photo of Lulu, Kingsley, and me, Lulu's arm wrapped around my waist, all I can think is after this weekend I'll be in close quarters with Lulu for the next few days.

And I'm loving that and hating that at the same damn time.

Sort of like how I felt at Lulu's wedding.

11

LEO

Eight Years Ago

I sprawled across the lounge chair in our apartment in Hoboken, late at night. We were finished with cooking school, and I had scored my first corporate job, while Tripp had landed a gig as a sous-chef, and Lulu worked in an entry-level post with a boutique chocolatier.

"Another one. Give me another one," Lulu demanded from her spot on the leather couch that Tripp's dad had given him, another show-off gift. Her legs were draped over her soon-to-be-husband's.

"You're such a riddle junkie." He nuzzled her hair, kissing the top of her head. My chest tightened, but I'd learned to live with the ache.

"I'm a junkie, and Leo feeds my fix. It's that simple." She stared at me, bug-eyed, wiggling her fingers. "Bring it on."

I flipped to the next page in the book of riddles I'd

bought for her, a pre-wedding gift I'd given her that night. Because I was a glutton for punishment. Because she was a bright, bold, daring person I couldn't get enough of, even though I shouldn't be taking any hits of her.

"I lose my head in the morning and gain it at night. What am I?" I looked up as Lulu took a sip of her freshly poured glass of wine, considering the riddle. I chuckled to myself as I read the answer silently.

Tripp scrunched his brow. "A snake? Is it a snake?"

Cracking up, I rolled my eyes. "Do snakes lose their heads? Does your answer even make sense?"

He scoffed. "I bet there's some snake somewhere that loses its head. I'm sure if you looked in an encyclopedia of snakes, you'd find some weird-ass one that loses its head. Right, Lulu?"

She patted his thigh. "Tripp, I love you, baby, but you need to stop talking about snakes. I hate snakes. Even as an answer to a riddle. But it's not the answer. And let's hope there's not an encyclopedia of snakes anywhere."

"What's the answer, then, Miss Smarty Pants?" His hands darted to her waist, and he tickled her ferociously, igniting a flurry of laughter.

It was the full-bodied kind of chuckle that seemed to move through her like a wave, from her shoulders to her belly to her legs. "A pillow, you goofball."

He held up his hands in the air. "A pillow? A pillow loses its head in the morning?" He paused, then nodded. "Fine, it does. But, seriously. Who thinks of these things?"

"Let's just be glad someone does. Give me another, Leo."

"What comes once in a minute, twice in a moment, but never in a thousand years?"

Tripp cut in. "Did you get her a dirty book of riddles?"

I showed him the cover. "*101 Brain-Busting Riddles for the Riddle Lover in Your Life.*"

"Still sounds dirty."

"This one's easy," Lulu said to Tripp. "Think about it hard."

"If I'm thinking hard, then that is a dirty book of riddles."

"It's not dirty. I know what it is." Lulu practically bounced on the couch cushions, an eager student bursting with the answer.

Tripp furrowed his brow, then shrugged. "All I can figure is it's someone who starts out a stud but fails miserably."

Lulu thrust a fist in the air. "Nope. It's the letter *M*. Isn't that brilliant? It comes once in a minute, twice in a moment, but never in a thousand years."

"It is indeed brilliant," I said.

Tripp paused, processing the riddle, then laughed. "Good one."

He grabbed her wineglass and took a swig then set it back down on the table. "Listen, I'm man enough to admit I suck at riddles, but I am fucking awesome at feeding my woman." He rubbed Lulu's stomach. My jaw ticked, and I glanced at Lulu's wineglass. It was nearly half empty now. "You want some sautéed artichokes with shiitake mushrooms and polenta? I came up with this new recipe while I was riding my bike the other day, and it's going to make your stomach so happy that you jump me."

She arched a brow. "Your artichokes will make me jump you? That's what'll do it?"

"They'll make you come in a minute."

I groaned. Loudly.

"Oh, please. I heard what you did to Daphne the other night," Tripp said as he rose, mentioning the woman I'd been dating.

"Is that so?" I asked.

Tripp pumped his hips. "She was like, *oh Leo, oh Leo, oh Leo*. She was like that all night long." Lulu's eyebrows rose, and for a split second, I didn't mind that Tripp was imitating one of my lovers in the throes of passion. Let Lulu linger on *that* image. Tripp continued, talking to me, "Have I mentioned I can't wait to move in with my fiancée next week after she marries me? I can finally get away from you, Casanova."

He acted like I had a parade of women flitting into the place at all hours. I wasn't going to disabuse anyone of that notion.

Lulu sat up straighter, her lips quirking in curiosity. "You're a multiple man, Leo?"

Go out on a high note. Like George Costanza. I blew on my fingernails. "When you've got it, you've got it."

Lulu laughed. "I guess you've got it."

Tripp headed into the kitchen, and I returned to the book, reading more riddles to Lulu. That was my role with her. Riddle-supplier, not multiple-O-bestower.

"What has a tongue, but never talks, and has no legs, but sometimes walks?"

A beat. "A shoe."

"What belongs to you, but other people use it more than you?"

She hummed then her eyes lit up. "Your name."

Shortly after the next riddle, Tripp cursed from the kitchen. "Shit. I'm out of mushrooms. Be right back."

He took off for the store, and Lulu's stomach rumbled. "I'm hungry. I can't wait for him any longer. If I have to wait, my stomach is going to mutiny."

"Best to avoid that sort of insurrection."

"Don't tell Tripp I'm going to snack."

"It'll be our secret."

She grabbed a bag of popcorn, returned to the couch, and tossed a kernel into the air, catching it on her tongue. "I'm like a seal."

"Me too." I held open my mouth, and she tossed me one.

I caught it on the tip of my tongue and yanked it back, lizard-style. "Look at us. A couple of seals."

"We have so much in common."

"Because of that?"

She downshifted into serious mode. "No, but for other reasons. Think about it. We're both driven, we're both determined to succeed, we both work hard. And we both like Tripp. But I bet you can't wait for him to move out so you can have this place to yourself."

I couldn't wait, and I would also wait a thousand years if I could keep having her here like this. I was a Lulu junkie. I'd take the pain for the hit of pleasure.

"You ready for next week?" I asked, choking on the question, but needing to ask it just the same. The more

I stuck my finger in the flame, the less it would hurt when the skin burned.

"Yes. My mom's giving me away. Which is kind of against the grain, but I'm totally excited about it."

"It's always been just you and her. You two are so close. It's fitting that she does the honors."

"It feels right, you know? She's my family, and we're tight." She crunched on more popcorn, her expression turning somber, a touch of sadness in those mismatched eyes. "I feel bad that Tripp's parents hate each other so much that they'll be on opposite sides of the room. I hate how his dad is constantly trying to buy his love with gifts, but never time. And he needles his ex-wife like he wants to wear Vivian down. We have to make sure they don't sit at the same table at the rehearsal dinner or the reception."

"Yeah, that sucks. Vivian's great, but I know she can't stand being near his dad. I wish they could be there *for* Tripp instead of *against* each other." I reached for more popcorn.

"That's something else we have in common. Even though your family is traditional and mine isn't, we both rely on them so much. I rely on my mom, and you on your parents and your brothers. But Tripp doesn't really have anyone to rely on."

"True." When he was a teenager, his parents had fought and fought until they finally divorced, and the intensity of the vitriol was hard as hell on him.

She leaned closer to me, her eyes big and vulnerable. "That's why we have to look out for him, Leo. We're the family he wants. Promise me. Promise me that you and I will look out for him."

I swallowed hard, past the bile of my own guilt. "He's like a brother to me. I'll always look out for Tripp."

"I love that you see him that way. That's how I see you guys too, and it makes me happy. You're best friends, but you're also brothers."

"We are." It was the truth, and a necessary reminder.

When he came home a little later, he finished the mushrooms and polenta, served us an amazing dinner, and cracked open a new bottle of wine. Lulu insisted we dance and toast to the sounds of Bruno Mars.

I called Daphne, and she joined us, and that made the rest of the night more bearable.

I didn't ask her to come to the wedding with me though.

I couldn't ask anyone else to endure being my plus-one at what was both a celebration and a funeral.

* * *

A week later, Tripp adjusted his bow tie in the hotel suite. "What do you think? Am I a handsome devil or what?"

I met his gaze in the mirror. "I'm not going to answer that."

"C'mon, don't I look good?"

"Yeah, jackass. Like a penguin."

He smacked my back, laughing. "If I look like a penguin, what do you look like?"

I considered my tux, same as his except for the cummerbund. "Best man?"

"You're like the runner-up penguin."

I winced inside. He had no idea. "Let's stick with best man."

He smiled, a big, genuine one. "All right. Time to go marry the love of my fucking life." He turned to me, tugging on his cuffs even though they were neat, his smile slipping away. "You know Lulu is the best thing that ever happened to me, right?"

My heart lurched. In moments like this, Tripp *was* my brother, shedding all his lightness, all his masks. "I know that, man."

"I love her like crazy."

"I know you do."

"She's the only thing in my life that's made sense. Well, besides cooking. But you know what I mean?"

He was talking about his family. "I know what you mean."

He stepped closer, emotion straining his voice. "I want to do right by her. My whole life."

The guilt lassoed my waist, yanking tighter. But I'd done nothing wrong by loving her. I'd never acted on it. I shouldn't feel so much damn guilt. *Just be his friend, like you've always been*, I told myself. "You will, Tripp. You will."

"You really think I'm good enough for her?"

"She said yes to you. She loves you. Go make her happy."

He exhaled deeply. "She makes me so happy."

We left the suite and headed to the small ballroom where a justice of the peace waited.

I entered with him, the knot twisting and turning in me like a tornado.

Best man, best man.

I needed to behave like the best man.

And the best man should not be madly in love with the bride.

When Pachelbel's Canon in D played, the attendees rose, all eyes on the woman in white as she walked down the aisle to marry my best friend.

I knew it would hurt.

I wasn't prepared, though, for how sharply it would sting when I finally raised my gaze. It was like my insides were being excavated as I watched Lulu, radiant in a strapless dress that showed off delicate shoulders I wanted to kiss in another lifetime. She walked down the aisle beaming, her mother's arm in hers, the way she had wanted.

Her eyes stayed on the groom. Never wavering.

He never wavered either.

Thank God all eyes were on them. No one was looking at the best man. In case anyone did, I schooled my expression so the emotions would read like pride and joy, rather than one last fleeting wish that she was walking to me.

When she joined him, he smiled and whispered, "You look so pretty."

He was wrong though. She was breathtakingly beautiful.

And never more so than when she pledged to love him *till death do us part.*

I took my own vow that day. No matter what, I had to get over her. There were no runners-up in love.

Present Day

The next evening I'm practically bouncing off the walls, prepping for the scavenger hunt. The level of fired up I feel might be off the charts. I text Leo.

Lulu: I'm stretching.

Leo: I'm listening to an audiobook on the wonders of Brazil. But I'll bite. Why are you stretching?

Lulu: It's prep work for the hunt. Did you know I'm completely determined to take home the prize?

Leo: I had a feeling you were. And so you anticipate

needing to stay flexible while engaged in a team-building Easter-egg-of-sorts hunt?

Lulu: You never know what hoops we might need to jump through! My friend Mariana told me her law firm tried team building once, and the big boss threw all sorts of unexpected stuff their way.

Leo: Such as?

Lulu: He made them do things together. Like have meals. And discuss their feelings. Gag.

Leo: Sounds horrendous.

Lulu: They're lawyers, so you can imagine how well that went.

Leo: As well as finding a parking place in the theater district on a Saturday night?

Lulu: Who would even attempt such an impossibility?

Leo: No one, Lulu. Absolutely no one. What other prep work are you doing?

Lulu: Why? Angling to join me?

Leo: I don't think you want to see me in leg warmers doing calisthenics.

Lulu: Was that even an option? Either the calisthenics or the leg warmers?

Leo: Shockingly, no.

Lulu: Fine. We shall work on our brain stretching. I'm seeing my mom later tonight. Want to meet me at An Open Book in fifteen minutes?

Leo: I'll bring my brain along.

Lulu: It's good that you keep it handy like that. PS What are the wonders of Brazil? Besides chocolate.

Leo: I'll tell you when I see you shortly.

13

LULU

The second he strides down the aisle at An Open Book on Saturday night, he announces, "It's tucked into the corner of Argentina, Brazil, and Paraguay."

I search my brain, but it goes blank. I'm good with riddles, not geography.

"Tell me what this wonder is."

"The two hundred seventy-five falls of Iguazu. One of the most stunning waterfalls in the entire world."

He whips out his phone and shows me a stunning image of water pouring over cliffs at sunset, and it takes my breath away. "That is definitely a natural wonder."

He gives me a satisfied smile. "Your turn."

I rub my palms. "Riddle time. It's shorter than the rest, but when you're happy, you raise it up like it's the best. What is it?"

Leo hums, his dark-brown eyes deep in thought. As his brow furrows, it's as if I can see the cogs in his brain whirring. "I want to say flagpole, but that makes no sense."

I rock back and forth on my wedge sandals. "Definitely not a flagpole."

"Happy." He seems to turn the word over in his hands. "Raise it up." He stares at the shelves beyond my head. "When you're happy, you raise the roof, you raise your arms, you raise your . . ." Leo's smile spreads, that warm and buzzy kind of smile that makes the air crackle, as he lifts his hand and in slow motion raises the shortest digit. "Thumb."

I thrust my arms into the air in victory, then set the book down on the shelves. "You are a riddle master."

"Hardly. Just analytical."

I give him a *duh* look. "Yes, that's what it takes to solve riddles."

"And that would make *you* analytical?"

I tilt my head. "Yes, I'm analytical. Why does that seem like such a surprise?"

"Well, lady in sequins, I wonder." He gestures to my red sequined tank top that slopes off one shoulder, my skinny jeans, and my silver sandals. "Analytical is not the first adjective I'd use to describe you."

I park my hands on my hips, considering his monochrome wardrobe—dark jeans and a gray T-shirt that hugs his pecs and shows off arms that are stronger than I remembered. Or maybe I never noticed his arms before. "Then what adjective is the one you'd use, Mr. Black-and-White Wardrobe?"

He mimics me, setting his hands on his hips. "Rainbow-loving."

"That's not an—" I let my shoulders fall dramatically. "Damn, that *is* an adjective." I poke his shoulder.

"But why can't color lovers be analytical, you pigeon-holer, you?"

"Actually, they can. When you think about it, it makes perfect sense that you're a riddle lover. It's analytical, and creating recipes is too."

"Exactly. I'm so damn analytical, you're going to call me Miss Analysis from now on. Except confession: I hate spreadsheets."

"Confession: I love them."

"Spreadsheet lover," I tease, enjoying the back-and-forth with Leo. We've always exchanged rapid-fire words, and it feels so natural, so right to slide back into that kind of repartee. "To each his or her own. Also, should we look at more riddle books or don leg warmers and do calisthenics?"

"No to the latter. As for the former? You do realize it's not a riddle contest?"

I glare at him. "If it's not, it should be."

"Nor is it a hide-and-seek contest. You were touting your prowess in that to Kingsley."

"But that would be so fun. Hey, maybe we could join a hide-and-seek league. I bet Noah would be all over that."

"I've no doubt he'd be all over *any* league."

"Do you think hide-and-seek leagues truly exist?"

"If I were betting, I'd say yes. There are leagues for hacky sack and Monopoly, so I suspect you'd find one for hide-and-seek."

I glance around the bookstore, bustling with evening shoppers out hunting celebrity biographies, travel guides, sudoku puzzles, and more, then whisper, "Let's practice. See if you can find me."

I dart around the brainteasers and into the neighboring section of cookbooks, Leo's laughter trailing behind me. In exaggerated fashion, I duck. Seconds later, he taps my shoulder. "Tag, you're it."

"We're playing tag now too?" I set my hand on my chest. "Be still, my beating heart."

"Lulu, is there a game you don't love?"

I stand, raising my chin defiantly. "I had a very rich and fulfilled childhood. Don't mock me for liking to have fun."

Laughing, he shakes his head. "Consider yourself thoroughly unmocked."

"Great. And I'm holding you to a pin-the-tail-on-the-donkey game at some point."

"I will consider it a date." He stops short on that last word, as if it's strangling him. "I mean, I'll consider it—"

I touch his arm, wanting to remove any weirdness he feels. "I know what you mean."

He meets my gaze, saying nothing. The air pulses between us. And maybe this evening here in the bookstore, laughing, teasing, playing, does feel the slightest bit like a date.

And maybe I like how it feels.

That realization clobbers me from out of nowhere. But it shouldn't. I've always liked spending time with Leo. I shouldn't be surprised that I enjoy his company.

I simply need to remind myself that this is Lulu and Leo 101. We've taken this class. We know the curriculum cold.

We check out some more brain-busting books, since I'm convinced that'll help us win the scavenger hunt, and when we're done, we wander through the aisles. I run my finger along the shelves, savoring the feel of the wood, then the spines of the books. "I don't think I'll ever be an e-reader gal. Is that terrible to say?" I grab a book, open it, and sniff the pages. "I love the smell of books."

"Doesn't surprise me."

"Why?"

"You're a tactile person."

"Am I?"

"Of course you are. You're attuned to your senses. Your eyes seek out color, your hands are drawn to ingredients, your taste buds crave chocolate."

"Speaking of . . ." I dip my hand into my purse then bring a finger to my lips. "Shh. I brought you a sample. Don't tell a soul."

He hums. "Gimme. Now."

I hand him a chocolate square, and he drops it on his tongue. He sighs as he chews, taking his time, savoring the flavors, it seems. "Lulu, this is decadent."

"You really like it?"

"I love it. It has a hazelnut taste, but then it's strong too, with the darker chocolate. Is that from Brazil?"

I nearly squeal. "Yes. That's amazing that you can tell."

"I have good taste buds," he says, in a whisper that's a little naughtier than I expected. "Would you make me a secret stash?"

"For you, I would."

His expression shifts like he's studying my face, and the veracity of my answer. "You would?"

I slug his shoulder. "Of course I would. I'd do nearly anything for you."

"Nearly, huh?"

"Oh, stop. When people say they'd do *anything* for someone, it's never true. Rarely would someone do literally anything."

"Is this one of those times when you're talking about something other than what you're saying?"

"What do you mean?" I ask, confused.

"Is this you still feeling like you didn't do enough for Tripp?"

I hit pause in the self-help aisle to think about his question. In general, I try to be up-front and direct. But with Leo, I feel like I can't be anything but that. He knows me so well. He's seen me incandescently happy, devastatingly sad, and everything in between. I wear my heart on my sleeve, and he knows it.

But in this case, he's wrong. "No. I know I did enough. I have no regrets." That's honestly one of the greatest feelings ever—to be free of the past.

The smallest sliver of a smile plays on his lips, then it disappears as if he won't permit it to stay. "Good. Because you did. We both did. How is it being back in New York?"

"You mean because it's where Tripp and I used to live?"

"That's one of the reasons you went to California, right?"

"I needed to get away at the time. I'm glad I did, but I'm happy to be in New York. Honestly, everything that happened with Tripp is behind me." I say it like I mean it because I do. It took time and effort and introspection, but I've moved on. But has Leo? Something in his eyes, a sadness perhaps, makes me wonder. "What about you? Have you moved on?"

He scoffs like my question is crazy. "Of course. You can't live in the past."

When I look at Leo, I see a man who's accomplished so much, who set out to chase his dreams and who achieved them. He wasn't waylaid or sidetracked like I was, and I admire his tenacity.

"And you can't live for someone else," I add.

"You took the words right out of my mouth." His gaze catches on his watch, then his lips part in an O. "Hate to end this, but I think you said you're meeting your mom for dinner in ten minutes?"

And I hate the thought of this evening with him ending. "Come with me?"

14

LULU

You know how tunics became popular with tweens? How they all started wearing long shirts over their yoga pants?

Those girls have nothing on Tabitha Diamond.

No one rocks a tunic like my mother.

She owned that look before it became trendy. She's paired her clingy black top, cinched with a silver chain-link belt, with slinky leggings and black ankle boots. The woman defies age. Her dyed blonde hair—obviously it's dyed, she likes to say with a knowing grin—is cut pixie-short.

She rises from her spot at the restaurant bar, embracing me then turning to Leo and clasping his shoulders. "Look at you."

"How do I look?"

"Like someone we need to see more of."

Leo laughs then drops a kiss to her cheek. "Pleased to see you again, Miss Diamond."

She waves a hand affectionately. "Oh, I love you. Thank you for calling me 'Miss.'"

"You forbade me long ago to ever call you 'ma'am' or 'madam' or 'Mrs.'"

"And you remembered."

He taps his skull. "Your daughter makes me work my brain."

My mom turns to me with an approving nod. "And I made her work hers, even when watching TV."

I hold up a finger to make a point. "Especially when watching TV."

She shifts instantly into professorial mode. "When you watch it with a critical eye, you can study people, psychology, and human interaction. More so, we can understand the images that shape our world and perception."

"Have I mentioned my mother teaches media and culture?" I tease.

"I had no idea," Leo jokes.

"I can go on and on, and I will. Just giving you fair warning. But, Leo, just call me Tabitha."

He nods. "I'll do that . . . Tabitha."

She smiles, gathers her bag, closes her tab, and gestures to a table. "Come, sit. The host held us this table when Lulu told me you were coming."

"Thanks for letting me crash your dinner."

"You're the kind of dinner crasher I welcome."

"And what kind is that, Mom?" I take my seat in one of the bright blue chairs at the table.

My mom winks. "Someone who's entertaining. I can't abide boring dinner guests. That's my hard limit."

"It's good to have standards," Leo says dryly.

She drums her short, unpolished fingernails on the table as she looks at Leo. "Tell me everything. How have you been? How is work? How's life?"

The two of them chat after the waiter drops by to take our drink order, and I listen, enjoying the ease of their interaction, enjoying, too, that Leo thanks the waiter and so does my mom. They dive right into conversation, volleying with a steady cadence. When appetizers arrive, my mom tastes the shrimp and rolls her eyes. "You have to try this."

I take a bite, and it melts on my tongue. "Fantastic."

She holds out her fork to Leo. "And you."

"Delicious."

Between courses, she returns her focus to Leo. "How is your mom doing? Is she still making the most beautiful arrangements of irises and lilies in all of Philadelphia? When I led a symposium there a few years ago, I stopped by and ordered a bouquet from her to thank the organizers. She looked lovely and well."

Leo smiles warmly. "She's great. She mentioned you'd stopped by. She said, and I quote, 'Lulu's mom is a total delight, and I can see why you—'" Leo slams the brakes on that word, then takes a sharp right. "'I can see why Lulu is the way she is.'"

I stare at him quizzically, as if I can will him to say what he intended, but his eyes are impassive.

My mother laughs, sets a hand on my arm, and squeezes. "Lulu is the way she is because she's an amazing woman."

"Raised by an amazing woman," I add, but even as

they chat more, my brain keeps snagging on his unfinished sentence—*I can see why you ...*

Why he what?

"What is she up to now?" my mother inquires.

"She retired a year ago, along with my dad. I helped them pay off their mortgage, so they don't have to worry about that."

My heart warms instantly. "Leo," I say softly.

"What?"

"That's so sweet."

"Your parents must be so proud of you," my mother chimes in. "That's a very lovely gift to give them. The gift of no longer worrying."

"It's the least I could do."

"And your two brothers?"

"I saw them a few weekends ago. Took in a Phillies game. Owen works in retail, and Matthew manages a hotel. They're doing well. Matthew's wife is expecting."

My eyes light up. "When is the baby due?"

He squints as if he's thinking. "About three more months, I think."

"Lulu has always been good with little kids. At the park she used to play with younger children, helping them down the slides or on the swings."

Leo smiles like it contains a whole galaxy. "Is that so? You were like a camp counselor at the park."

"And then I *was* a camp counselor. I always liked kids. They were easy to get along with."

My mom pats my shoulder, stage-whispering, "And they always loved her clothes. Especially when she wore purple tutus and pink tiaras along with her cowgirl vests."

"Mix and match was my jam," I admit. "Don't forget I had cowgirl hats to go with everything too."

"Pink, purple, red, and green cowgirl hats," my mom adds.

Leo stares at me, grinning. "What other outfits did she have, Tabitha?"

My mom regales Leo with more tales of me as a tot, then as a tween and teen, and he seems to eat it all up. After they crack up over a story about me wearing tiaras to school every single day in third grade, my mom downshifts, taking a drink of her wine. The twinkle in her eyes flickers off, turning dark. "Have you heard from Tripp's mother lately? Is she still fundraising?"

Leo nods. "We chatted a few months ago. She was starting to organize a 10K, I believe, for an addiction awareness and advocacy group. I actually need to connect with her again, especially since we've been playing phone tag lately."

My mom sighs sympathetically. "Bless her. She's taken a terrible thing and done her best to make some good of it."

The mention of her makes my throat hitch. I haven't seen her since the funeral, and she lives in Manhattan, relocating here after spending most of her life in Virginia. I ought to look her up, but then again, what would I say?

Mom wipes her eyes, her voice wobbly. "I can't even imagine what she went through."

"*Hell.* She went through hell," I answer quietly, an invisible fist squeezing my heart as an image of Tripp's mother, grief-stricken, breaking down into piercing sobs at the memorial service, blasts cruelly before me. Her husband comforted her as best he could, but there's no comfort for that kind of loss. No salve for her wounds.

Later that day, she set a gentle hand on my shoulder, her voice stretched to the edge of sorrow. "Thank you for trying."

"I'm sorry it wasn't enough."

A tear threatens to escape, but I keep it at bay.

Mom turns to me. "I don't ever want anything to happen to you, okay, baby?"

I fasten on a smile, willing away the tears and the memories. "I'll do my best to live. And to live well."

"It's all you can do." She reaches for her glass. "Let's drink to moderation."

"Amen," we all say together.

When Leo clinks his glass to mine, his gaze lingers on me. "To living well."

"To going after what you want," I add, a strange little flutter in my chest.

"To chasing your dreams," my mother adds. "And to finding them."

She looks to Leo once more. "You're a dream chaser. A go-getter. Have you found your dreams?"

I watch Leo, eager for his answer, searching for it in his expression. At times like this, he's nearly impossible to read, even as I study the cut of his jaw, the darkness in his eyes.

"Most of them. Some slipped away though."

He sounds so wistful and resigned that I want to dig

in, ask him what slipped away, and comfort him. Instead, I say, "Then you make new dreams."

* * *

Before the food arrives, Leo excuses himself for the men's room. My mom tips her chin in his direction. "My, he is like a fine wine. Did he get better with age or what?"

"Mom, stop it."

"I'm not allowed to say if a man is good-looking?"

"Are you making a play for Leo?"

She scoffs. "Please."

"Are you?"

"I'm fifty years old, and I'm very happily enjoying my thirty-five-year-old boyfriend, thank you very much."

"How is it that you have a thirty-five-year-old boyfriend?"

"Pilates."

I laugh then look her over. She's gorgeous and always has been. And she's never flaunted it. "You're ridiculously hot for any age."

"That's because I don't believe there's anything wrong with being fifty and sexy. You only live once. Make the most of it. Be beautiful. Be your best beautiful self." She smooths her hand over her napkin. "But why were you so worried if I was making a play for Leo?" Her question drips with curiosity. "Are *you* making a play for him?"

It's my turn to scoff. "Please."

"It's not out of the realm of possibility."

"Tabitha." I use her first name to make it clear I don't want her to go there. I can't go there because of the past, and I can't go there because of the present.

"Seriously, Lulu. I always did like him, but I'm not merely talking about his looks. He has a good head on his shoulders."

"He does."

She taps her chin. "For a fleeting second at the table, he looked at you like . . ."

She trails off, but I pounce on her statement. "Like what?"

"Like you were . . ."

Again, she doesn't finish. But she needs to finish. She *must*. I have to know how he looks at me. I'm wildly compelled, and I don't even understand why. "You're never at a loss for words. He looked at me like what?"

"Like there were years in his eyes."

"You mean stars, right?"

"I know the saying about stars in their eyes. I meant years."

The word burrows into my cells. *Years.*

There are years between us. A whole decade of friendship, challenges, sadness, and now, new hope in a new era of friendship. But I don't think she means it that way. Trouble is, I don't know what to make of how she means it. "That's insane."

"I know you're friends, but I swear there was something there. I swear, Lulu." She studies my face for a moment, humming. "And I saw how you looked at him too."

"And how exactly did I look at him?" I challenge her.

"Like there's something there that wasn't there before."

"Did you just go *Beauty and the Beast* on me?"

She laughs. "I suppose I did."

I shake my head, like I can dismiss these crazy notions in a single gesture. My dismissal works as a shield too. "And you should know, it'll never happen with him."

She arches an eyebrow. "People say that, and then it happens."

"Seriously, you need to just stop talking." I stick out my tongue at her, deflecting. The ideas she's presenting are . . . dangerous. "Because that's not going to happen."

The more I say it, the more it'll stick with me.

"Your lips say one thing, but your eyes say another."

Exasperated, I toss up my hands. "He's good-looking. There's that."

"Who's good-looking?"

My shoulders straighten, and my face feels like it turns every shade of red as Leo returns to his seat.

Undeterred, my mom arches a brow at him. "You. She meant you."

A grin hijacks his face. "Well, thank you."

He doesn't seem to stop smiling, not as we eat, not as we talk, not as we laugh and catch up and my mom shares stories of her new students and her boyfriend and the life she's living so richly now.

As she's always done.

Even when her life turned upside down when she was pregnant with me at eighteen, she never stopped pursuing her dreams. And she's never stopped encouraging me to live my best life.

Right now, right here, this is the closest I've come in a long time to feeling like I might be on that path.

Something else occurs to me too. Even though we've never done this before—dinner with Leo, my mom, and me—it feels like old times. Like good times. Like no one is waiting for the other shoe to drop at the end of the night.

When the evening ends, my mother says good night and heads home. Leo takes the subway with me then walks me to my apartment.

As we near the stoop, time seems to mock me.

I want to stop the clock. To live in this moment where everything feels possible. Where the evening won't need to end.

So I lap up the last few seconds of tonight, looking at Leo. The moonlight sketches his face, illuminating his cheekbones, his eyes. I like the way his hair falls, how his gaze hooks on me, how his lips part softly when he speaks. I look at him in a whole new way.

That way terrifies me.

For a million reasons.

I choose the well-worn path, the friendly one that's familiar. "Wednesday morning. You, me, and the team. We'll be ready to own this scavenger hunt."

"So ready."

"Like we better be."

"The readiest."

"Good night, Leo." I lean in and give him a quick kiss on the cheek, and for a hair's breadth of a second, I swear I hear a hitch in his breath.

Or maybe it's in mine.

When we separate, he gives me that lazy, handsome

grin. "So you think I'm good-looking?" His dark eyes twinkle with something like desire.

Tingles spread their wings and fly down my chest, then soar to the night sky. "I'm not blind, Leo."

We say good night.

I turn around and don't look back because of all those millions of reasons.

15

LEO

I don't go home. I head to the warehouse and work on an old chair I unearthed in Croton-on-Hudson. I strip the veneer off the arms, the repetitive motion quieting my wild thoughts until my arms are exhausted.

The work centers me, and after the enchanted evening with Lulu, I'm feeling anything but steady.

When I return to my place overlooking Central Park, I shower as the clock hits midnight, then I flop down on my bed and grab my phone.

One last check.

Or maybe one dangerous hope.

I'm hoping for a text from Lulu.

Which is dumb as fuck. We're not *good night, sweetie pie* people. She won't send me a *had a nice night* text. That's not what this is. That's not who we are to each other.

Instead, I find a voicemail from Tripp's mom, since we've been trying to reach each other, then a text from

Dean, followed by an email from Kingsley telling me the hunt's a little bigger than we had first planned.

I swear I can hear the boss lady chuckling over cyberspace. The woman is a hoot, and I'm a lucky bastard to work for someone who has a big heart, big wallet, and big sense of FUN, all caps for sure.

Turns out the hunt has supersized, with ten companies competing for the prize pack:

A ten-thousand-dollar donation to the winning team's charity of choice.

A spa day, or a day at the golf course.

And last, but definitely not least, a paid week off for the winning team's division.

Let the record reflect, there is no better incentive for any employee anywhere in the world than the prize of less work.

I write back to her, letting her know I'll do my damnedest to make her proud, then write to Dean, giving him the gist of Kingsley's update since he finds corporate life amusing. I email Tripp's mom since it's too late to call.

But they're not the ones I'm thinking of as my head hits the pillow, nor are they on my mind when the pillow gives up my head the next morning.

My mind is a tsunami of thoughts, emotions, and memories all day Sunday as I finish the chair, and then into Sunday night as I chat with my brothers on the phone. I have to quiet these Lulu-tinged thoughts before work begins in earnest this week.

But I've never been terribly good at kicking her out of my mind, no matter how hard I've tried.

* * *

At the crack of dawn, I tug on basketball shorts, a T-shirt, and running shoes, then hit the park, toggling over to a podcast on the current ecology of the Galapagos Islands. Focusing on my personal educational goals is the ideal balm for the storm in my head.

Midway through the highlands inhabited by giant tortoises, Dean texts.

Dean: Rah rah. Go, team, go. Can you hear me rooting for you all the way across town?

Leo: With amazing enthusiasm and incredible clarity. Do you have pom-poms too?

Dean: For you, I'd consider it.

Leo: I'm honored that you take my corporate pursuits so seriously.

Dean: Oh, please. It's not you. We started a betting pool at The Pub last night. We have all sorts of wagers going on for the Crisps vs. Chocolate scavenger hunt.

Leo: Chips, dude. Chips.

Dean: Two words I will never utter. "Chips" and "dude." *shudders*

Leo: I'll Americanize you in no time, bro.

Dean: And yet another.

Leo: Anyway, how much did you bet on me?

Dean: Did I say I bet on you?

Leo: Ah. Should have known you wouldn't bet on me.

Dean: What do you expect? Once I got word that it had spiraled beyond those two companies and somehow, mind-bogglingly, had become all of the packaged food firms in New York, what was I to do? Deny myself the chance to bet on a stallion?

Leo: And who is your stallion?

Dean: Anyone but the guy on the team with the girl he once fancied.

As I crest a hill, I find the middle finger emoticon and send it back to him. If I were him, I'd poke fun at me too.

I keep up a steady clip through the park. A guy who looks familiar tears past me, seeming hell-bent on racing to the edge of the world.

Like a car whips around in a U-turn, the guy zips

back to me. It's Noah. He's slowed to a jog at my side. "Whoa. Thought it might be you, big man."

"You can just call me Leo."

"Dude, you're a fucking EVP. I'm a director of sales. You're the big man in charge, even if we're in different departments."

"Hate to break it to you, but there's a woman in charge."

"Ha. Good point." He smacks my arm. "Hey, you're friendly with Ginny, right?"

"I am."

"You know her well then?"

"Well enough. She's a colleague and a friend."

He slides into a Hispanic accent. Mexican, I think. "Question then. Do you think I should lean on my natural Latino flare with her?"

I stare at him in question. "Um, you've literally never used that accent before."

"Yeah, because I grew up in New York. But I can pull it off. My whole family is from Mexico. And I am fluent, bi-lingual, and hella sexy. Like Michael Peña."

"I'm going to take the fifth on the last point. To the first, yes you absolutely can pull off the accent. I'm just not sure it's necessary since she knows you as you."

"So you don't think she likes a sexy, seductive accent?"

"No idea. But I think you should be yourself."

His voice turns earnest. "Fair enough. Think you could put in a word for me? Let her know I'm a good guy?"

"Why can't you do that yourself?"

"Please. I need to wear her down. It's the only way a woman like her will go for a guy like me."

"A guy who sees himself as Michael Peña?"

"And that dude scores. But no, I mean someone she works with."

I'm not sure if the specter of an office romance is the issue with Ginny, or if she has one, or if she even likes Noah, or *Michael Peña* for that matter. I give Noah the best advice I can. "Just ask her out, man."

"Yeah?"

"Yeah. It's simple. Only way you'll know."

He strokes his goatee as he trots. "You're right. Damn, you're always right. Also, no offense, big man, but you're slow as shit. I need to go full cheetah."

Laughing, I wave as he takes off like he has spots.

With Noah already on another continent, I return to the thread with Dean, rereading his last note, then his follow-up to it.

Dean: Anyone but the guy on the team with the girl he once fancied.

Dean: You see, I'm betting you'll be a wee bit distracted.

Leo: Distraction is for wusses. I have a powerful mind-vise, and I'm not afraid to use it.

Dean: Fair enough. So, speaking of things you put in mind-vises, how is our fair maiden?

The answer arrives as swiftly as a Bugatti.

Lulu is mesmerizing, she's charming, and she's enchanting.

It's as if I'm getting to know her all over again. Like we're having conversations for the first time, talks that exist only between the two of us, and I don't have to worry about crossing any lines with my best friend. Though, in the back of my mind, I'm vaulting over all the boundaries.

The woman is still off-limits, and that's not merely because of that tangled skein of history stretching between us across the years.

It's because I'd be a stupid ass to pursue something with a woman I now have a business deal with.

We're team building, not team fucking. I want this partnership to be successful, and success won't come from distraction.

Yet as my sneakers pound against the dirt path, I can't stop thinking about last night.

The caveman part of me—hell, all of me—loves that she thinks I'm good-looking. I feel a little bit like Rudolph the Red-Nosed Reindeer did when Clarice told him he was cute. I could go skipping and jumping and flying into the air. *She thinks I'm cute, she thinks I'm cuuuuuuuuuuute.*

But I can't say that aloud, for fuck's sake.

And honestly, I should relinquish my man card for a full twenty-four hours for even letting myself think it. In fact, I'd like to slap my brain for suggesting that

Rudolph the fucking Red-Nosed Reindeer and I have anything in common.

I'm not Rudolph.

I'm Iron Man.

I'm impervious to Lulu.

I'm stoic and tough as motherfucking nails.

Just to prove it, I reply to Dean's *how is Lulu* question with a curt *great*.

I exit the park, slowing to a fast walk as I hit the cobbled sidewalk.

Dean: She's great, as in a great conversationalist? Great contortionist? Great lady? Great time? Elaborate, mate. You're killing me.

Leo: Great friend.

As I weave past fellow New Yorkers speed-walking to work, I stare at that lie.

The last time I felt anything for Lulu, there was no one I could turn to, so I choked down all my emotions. I didn't utter a word of my feelings to anyone until much later on, when I vomited up the pathetic truth to Dean one night over beer at a hockey game.

As that memory rises, another one does too— telling Dean helped me breathe again. To unknot the noose of emotion around my neck.

I want to move forward, not backward.

Reaching the corner, I tap out a text.

Leo: Actually . . . let me be brutally honest. I meant, great in the sense that . . . hell. You know what I mean.

My phone rings instantly.

Dean wastes no time. "Where is this coming from?" His tone is earnest, thoughtful. It reminds me that maybe I don't need to process these new twists alone.

Besides, just because I once had monster feelings for Lulu doesn't mean that these new ones are poised to become the same size. Hell, this pitter-patter of emotions is merely a petering-out tropical storm, a category-five hurricane that's been downgraded multiple times.

"We just . . . we spent a little time together. Had dinner with her mom."

"Oh. Dinner with the mum."

"It's not a big deal."

"But is it? Is it really no big deal? Time hasn't entirely erased the way you feel for her."

"It has," I insist as I try to sort out the remains of the storm. "It's different now."

"It's different because she's actually single."

She's been single for a few years now. She wasn't always married to Tripp.

16

LULU

Three years ago

When I left for work on a warm April morning, I reminded Tripp it was a half day for me. "Don't forget to meet me at the eye doctor this afternoon for my Lasik appointment."

"I will be there to service all of your needs, my lady."

"Mostly you just need to sign me out so I'm not stuck spending the night there."

"No soon-to-be-eagle-eyed wife of mine will spend the night stuck in a Lasik surgery center."

Tripp met me in Midtown that afternoon and was with me when I checked in, signing the requisite form that he'd be there to take me home too.

The surgeon was running behind. Tripp said he was going to grab a coffee while they gave me new eyes.

I encouraged him to get a cup. He was antsy and

easily distracted. He kissed me goodbye, said he'd be back in no time, and joked that he'd be even better looking when I had my new eyesight.

The procedure began late. It ended after six.

He wasn't in the waiting room.

Embarrassment clung to me like bad perfume. They wouldn't let me leave alone. The nurses kept asking if anyone else could take me home.

"I'll get a cab."

That wasn't acceptable. I needed a person. They wouldn't let me leave without a human by my side.

Tripp didn't answer his phone, and I thought about calling my mom, or calling Leo, but they worked on opposite ends of the city. I was close to Mariana's building, and she always worked late.

"Can you come get me and sign me out like I'm in grade school?" I tried to make it sound light.

She told me she'd be there in ten minutes.

She arrived in eight, signed the discharge forms, and walked me to a waiting town car. Her regular car.

Once inside, she looked me over. "Sweetie, tell me one thing. What are we going to do about this?"

Her accent came out to play when she wasn't in court or at work. She liked to joke that she saved her all-neutral, no-nonsense voice for when she needed to scare other attorneys, but when she needed to give tough love to her friends, she was the girl from Puerto Rico.

I started to speak. To defend him. To say, *It's just one appointment. People forget.*

But I couldn't. I heaved a sigh. "What do I do?"

"Is this what you want? Is this what you signed up for? A man who doesn't keep his commitments?"

I jerked my gaze to the window, staring through the tinted glass at the sea of New Yorkers, wondering where my husband was among them.

A few minutes later, my phone rang.

"Where are you, babe? I'm here, looking for you. I was running late." I could *hear* the tequila on his breath.

Tears didn't come. Anger did. "Running late? You should have been running early. It was a cup of coffee and a phone call. That was all you had to do. Instead, Mariana is taking me home, and my vision is hazy, my eyes are bloodshot, and I'm wearing sunglasses at six thirty at night and it's April."

"I'm sorry. I got a call from a supplier, and I had to deal with it."

"I had something to deal with too."

"I'll make it up to you. I promise. I'll see you at home in a few minutes?"

"Obviously, you'll see me at home since that's where you were supposed to be taking me."

I ended the call. Tears welled up in my eyes. They weren't from the surgery.

"It's just Lasik. It's not a deal-breaker," I said.

Mariana arched a brow. "This may not be *the* deal-breaker. This may be forgivable. But it's not about this time. It's about the collective times. Think about the other times you've called me, wishing you were opening your own shop, wishing you had the time to open your own shop. But your time is all his. Think about where you want to be right now and how you want to get there."

"Are you saying I should leave him?"

She held up her hands as stop signs. "That is not my place. What I am saying is maybe it's time for some tough love."

A few weeks later, my eyesight was perfect. It was twenty-twenty, and the irony wasn't lost on me as I went to a kickboxing class with my new eyes.

With each punch, I counted. I still hadn't opened my chocolate shop, I was still paying bills that weren't mine, his restaurant was still struggling, and his loans were coming due.

Too many nights of him out late with his chef friends, coming home stinking of wine and tequila then crawling into bed, wanting to make love like that, needed to end.

We'd gone to therapy. We'd seen a counselor. I'd asked him to go to AA. He'd attended a few meetings. He'd earned his one-day sober chip five times over. And he'd lost it every time.

Five years after I said *I do*, I said something else. At the end of the workout, I turned to Mariana. "It's time."

She smiled. "You know I'm behind you, every step of the way."

That meant the world to me. That was the opposite of a deal-breaker.

I left class, called Leo, and asked him to meet me later that day for coffee.

* * *

At the coffee shop, Leo ordered a coffee with extra cream, just the way I liked it. He brought two mugs to the table. I clicked open the web page on my computer and toggled to the open tabs. "This one is nearby. I read about all its programs, and I think it can help him."

Leo peered at the screen, nodding as he read. "I'm no expert, but it sounds like a good choice."

"There are some others, but they're farther away and more expensive."

"I can pay for it." His eyes were flooded with hope and a strength that floored me. I didn't expect that. I didn't even think to ask for help, not from Leo and not from Tripp's parents. But Leo's willingness to do it, to put his money where his mouth was, stunned me.

"Thank you, but he's my responsibility."

He didn't answer right away. When he did, he pinned my gaze with his serious eyes. "He's *our* responsibility, Lulu."

A headache brewed out of nowhere behind my temples. I rubbed them, trying to rub away the pain. "He's my husband. I have to try."

"It's hard. It's harder on you than anyone else." That was all he said. All he needed to say. But he knew it. He understood.

"Paying for it is my responsibility. I took a vow, and I take it seriously."

"I know you do, but I'd like to help. I'd like to pay."

"No, thank you."

He sighed. "Tell me what I can do."

I inhaled and drew on all my strength, wavering though it was. But I had it in me. I had stores of it, thanks to my mom and the way I was raised. I'd been a strong girl growing up. I would be a strong woman. "I want us to tell him together. He'll do better if he knows we both want him to get well. That it's not just for me, but for you too."

"Strength in numbers. Of course."

"He loves me like crazy. But you, Leo? You're like his brother. He looks up to you. He needs to know it's hurting both of us. Most of all, though, he needs to know it's hurting him."

And so we planned. I talked to the rehab programs. I soaked up all the advice I could. I knew the risks. I knew the numbers and the high likelihood of a relapse.

But it needed to be done.

* * *

A few days later, I told Tripp I was sending him to a twenty-eight-day program. Leo stood by my side in the apartment I shared with the man I'd promised to cherish.

And dammit, I would. Helping him *was* cherishing him.

I sat Tripp down on the sofa. "I booked you into the program. You're leaving tomorrow."

He sputtered. "But what about the restaurant?"

Leo stepped in, brooking no argument. "I have it covered. I asked a sous-chef I know to fill in for you."

"But can he make all the dishes the same way? Can he handle the waiters? Can he handle—?"

"Yes."

That was all Leo said to the questions. *Yes.* He made it clear Tripp had no wiggle room on the work issue.

Tripp sighed heavily, sadness creeping over his face, but a newfound humility too. "Shit, man, you did that for me?"

"I'd do just about anything for you. And your wife would too. You need to know that."

Tripp's eyes welled with tears and gratitude. "Lulu, is this what you want?"

I got down on my knees, took his hands in mine. "Tripp, I want the man I married. I want you back. But I need you to do it for you."

"I will. I'll do it for me. I want to change. For you, and for me."

The next day Leo and I drove him to upstate New York. After Tripp checked in, he saluted me, his head held high. "I'm doing this. Thanks to you guys." He waved at us like a sailor boarding a ship bound to battle the enemy. No—to positively *vanquish* the enemy. "When you see me again, I'll be the king of seltzer water. We'll celebrate the new me with apple juice."

A sunflower bloomed inside me. A whole field. "Ginger ale and Diet Coke are the bomb."

"I can't wait to fill our fridge with 7 Up." He stopped in his tracks, pressing his fingers to his forehead. "I have an idea. I'm going to become a tea master. That's it! I'm going to be the reigning king of Earl Grey, jasmine green, and English breakfast."

"Don't forget oolong," I called out.

He ran back to me, cupped my cheeks. "Why can't we all just get oolong?"

I laughed so damn hard I nearly peed. This was the man I'd married. He'd be back. Just wait and see.

* * *

Two weeks later, he was kicked out of rehab for drinking. I didn't know how he got that bottle of Cuervo, but where there was a will, there was a way.

Three months later, I served him with divorce papers.

17

LEO

Present Day

In the middle of traffic-clogged, people-drenched Midtown Manhattan is a two-by-two-block park. You'd be hard-pressed to believe anything abutting Forty-Second Street could be peaceful, but Bryant Park is a hamlet in the middle of the metropolis, and on Wednesday morning, it's the epicenter of the hunt.

I emerge from the subway, aviator shades on, getting the lay of the land. As I walk toward the park, familiar faces come into view—some competitors, some business partners. Teams are ready, sporting their corporate gear in some cases, and in others they're wearing their casual best.

Draped in Jackie O sunglasses and nursing a coffee drink that's as tall as a baseball bat is Kingsley, her sister Scarlett by her side. The two women are laughing, a sign that this event has sprung from good-natured sibling rivalry.

But both are serious as sharks. You don't make it to the top of a major corporation without a little great white in you. Winning will make Kingsley happy. I like it when she's happy.

As I enter the park, a woman jogs toward me, her hair color so bright I have to squint, making it impossible to pretend I don't see her.

"Hey, RaeLynn." We met at an industry event a few years ago. She works at a candy company, and last year we were both vying for a partnership with a gourmet pretzel-maker.

The hyperblonde smiles; it's fierce and full of teeth, and her tone is oh so calculating.

"Leo, it's been ages. But I've totally forgiven you. Just kidding. I was never mad." She shoots me a *we're all good even though you beat me in the chocolate-covered-pretzel game* smile.

"I'm glad to hear I've received your absolution."

"Absolution. I love it. You were always a dictionary, weren't you?"

"I don't know. Was I?" I'm not sure what her agenda is, but I'm confident she has one. She's always had one.

She rolls her ice-blue eyes. "You were. And I'm sure you still are. Now, listen. I know we're going to compete, but I think we should let bygones be bygones. I've forgiven you for stealing my dream client."

"You know the facts. The business was up for grabs. I think we're good on this count, RaeLynn."

She laughs. "Fine, up for grabs. Have it your way."

"It's not about *my* way. It's how it was."

"It's water under the bridge. I'm not upset you won Pretzel-ology. Just like I'm sure you're not upset that we're launching a Hottest Young Stars line."

I let that little nugget sink in—that she's copycatting us. "Is that so?"

"Didn't you get my e-mail? I sent you one. You know I like to give you a heads-up." She wags a finger at me. "I bet it went to your spam. Leo, you need to check your spam."

"I check it religiously. Didn't see one."

"Anyhoo, maybe we can help each other on the hunt. The way I figure is if we both work together, and our teams both wind up with the same amount of points, or within five points of each other, we can both win, since I hear that's how the rules are structured. That way, we can ensure each of our groups gets a full week off."

Ah, the plot thickens like pea soup. Someone is currying favor with her employees. But I don't want to cozy up with this someone, since I don't trust her. "I'll think about that, RaeLynn."

She takes a step closer, lowers her voice to a throaty whisper. "This might be a chance for us to get to know each other better." She winks, and the agenda sharpens even more.

A throat clears. I follow the sound, and it's Lulu, looking delicious in shorts, sneakers, and a T-shirt that says *Life is too short to remove USBs safely*.

After I make quick introductions, RaeLynn eyes Lulu's shirt suspiciously. "You do know you should be careful with USBs, right?"

"I should?" Lulu acts shocked, and it's utterly delightful to watch.

"You're really not supposed to pull them out quickly."

Lulu's lips twitch, her eyes sparkle, and then words tumble from her mouth. "That's what she said."

I laugh heartily, and RaeLynn laughs obligatorily.

"Nice to meet you, RaeLynn."

"Nice to meet you too." She doesn't use Lulu's name, and the dig isn't lost on either one of us. "Anyway, think about my offer, Leo."

As RaeLynn strides away, Lulu stares at me, tapping her toe. "Let me guess. Little Miss Stick Up Her USB Butt was trying to convince you to team up with her?"

I laugh. "How could you tell?"

She shrugs. "Gosh, I have no idea. Also, I don't think she just wanted to team up with you for the hunt."

"You think she was making a play?"

She shoots me a *Silly Leo, Trix are for Kids* look. "I'm all for sisterhood and girl power, but that woman looked at you like she wanted to eat you up."

"And what does that look like?"

Parking her hands on her hips, straightening her shoulders, and jutting out her perky breasts, Lulu adopts the poutiest, sultriest look. When she's on this edge of caricature, she pushes herself over the line, making her lips look huge, Botoxed and bee-stung, before she puckers up.

Logically, she shouldn't look sexy right now. But the fact that she nailed RaeLynn's MO in seconds makes her sexy-smart, and her portrayal makes me laugh.

"Also, I don't want her making a play for you."

Make that sexy-smart and a little jealous. I *love* this look on her. "Are you jealous, Lulu Diamond?"

She takes my arm and links hers through it possessively. "You're *my* teammate. Mine, mine, mine."

It's a possessiveness born of friendship, but I like it. Because it doesn't feel the same as the first go-round. It's a little bit of the past, mixed with a lot of the present.

Still friends.

But a little flirty now.

Lulu was never flirty back then.

I like her flirty. I like her jealous. Everything feels like a new start, without a third person, without *me* as that third person.

A terrible fist of guilt claws at me out of nowhere, grappling my chest and telling me she's not just my best friend's girl, she's my *dead* best friend's girl.

It's one of my rules to live by.

Yet, here we are, walking together across this enclave in the middle of Manhattan. "Besides, I can't have you distracted by pretty girls. I need you focused."

That's an opening if I ever saw one. Before my mind clouds with lines crossed and codes broken, before regret lassoes me, I go for it. "If I'm distracted by pretty girls, you only have yourself to blame."

She stops, surprise etched in her eyes, both the green and the blue. "I do?" Her voice rises in question, as if she's opening the door a notch.

I kick it open, because screw regret. I don't have any this second. In fact, I'll regret it more if I don't speak my mind. "Just saying, I'm not blind." I step closer, studying her eyes, though I know them by heart. They're imprinted in my mind, in my soul. "By the way, I don't buy the green and not-so-green."

"You don't?"

Shaking my head, I run my finger across her cheekbone, beneath her right eye. Her breath catches. The sound emboldens me. "To me, one is the blue of the early morning sky, with flecks of green that almost, in certain light, give the illusion of this eye being pale green." I move my finger, tracing the line under her other eye, the movement rewarded by a tremble in her shoulders. "And the other is a cat's-eye green."

She's quiet as she raises her hand, her fingers fluttering across her cheek. "Really?"

"Yes, really. And they're beautiful."

She whispers a shuddery "Thank you," and the look on her face makes me feel like a king.

Sometimes you go against the rules.

* * *

The rules of the hunt?

Those, I intend to follow to the letter.

When it comes to games, sports, and work, cheating sucks.

Wait. Cheating sucks all the time.

But I'm not cheating on anyone or violating any bro codes, I tell myself.

A dark voice in my head whispers back, *You are, and you know it.*

As Kingsley and Scarlett rise majestically—the

sisters might as well wield scepters and don fur-lined robes—a voice in my head needles me.

What would Tripp say if he knew you were angling for his wife?

She's not his wife, I mutter privately to the insidious voice.

You're still his friend. That bond is stronger than death, the voice hisses.

I do my damnedest to quiet the voice as Kingsley reviews the rules of the hunt.

Ten teams are competing. Each will face three challenges, one on each of three successive days. Each challenge yields points. Teams will be given different clues, though most teams will wind up at the same general destination for each item, albeit searching for something different. You can't piggyback off another team to try to win. You need to figure out the clue, track down the item, and do the photo challenge to prove it, then return to the park, in most cases, to check in.

"Now, if you're thinking you can google the riddle, think again." Kingsley's voice booms. "One, that's seriously lame. Two, this is supposed to be fun. Three, see point number one. Four, and most important, take it to the bank, this is the God's honest truth: Google doesn't know everything."

"Take that back. Google is all-knowing," I tease, hoping to inject some levity into myself right now. Lord knows, I need it.

She shoots over a smile as a stocky guy in a golf shirt rubs his palms together, chiming in, "Who needs Google? I have a better incentive. The biggest one ever.

My wife made it clear I need to deliver a week of paid vacation. Or else. Mua ha ha ha."

"And what's the 'or else,' George?" Kingsley asks.

He shudders. "Have you met my wife? You don't want to mess with her . . . *or else*. No greater incentive for a man than a *honey, do, or else* order. Am I right or am I right?" He turns to me, eyebrows lifted, arms out.

Something about him is wildly familiar, and it dawns on me. He's the Finger-Licking-Good Guy, the one who said his wife would have him by the balls if he arrived home late. "Never disobey your commander in chief."

"Exactly."

Maybe I need to add that to my rules to live by.

Sure, you can replace the one you're bending, the voice whispers.

I square my shoulders and tell the voice to fuck the hell off.

This man is my levity. He's a character. I try to wind him up more, so I can coattail off his amusing attitude. "What would she do, though, do you think, if you didn't deliver on the *or else*?"

His face turns ashen. "Don't say such a thing. I don't want to know. You don't want to know. No one wants to know."

"Try me. I kind of do."

Under his breath, he whispers, "*The look*. She'll give me the look. And I value my existence, so I won't say any more."

I shudder on his behalf and pat myself on the back for successfully quieting the voice by drafting off George like I'm riding the edge of a wave.

I turn to my team, so I can focus on the task at hand. I motion for Ginny, Noah, and Lulu to huddle, taking the quarterback role. "Guys, let's concentrate. We want to win this because we love Kingsley, we like our jobs, and because we aren't dickweed, cutthroat bloodhounds who possess zero original ideas. Plus, our team would love a week off, and we'd love to win the money for charity. Wouldn't we?"

A chorus of "Yes, we would" comes from them, and we smack palms, energized.

When we separate from the huddle, Lulu smirks.

I take the bait. "What's so funny?"

"Your go-go-go side. It's cute."

My heart threatens to go Rudolph again, which is thoroughly unacceptable. I grab that reindeer's tail and pull him down to earth, donning my sarcasm deflector shield. "That's me. I'm a cutie-pie."

She squeezes my arm and smiles at me, so damn warmly. "Don't deny it. You're a total cutie-pie."

And the shield falls to the ground. "You too," I murmur.

Then George chimes in once more, whispering in a man-to-man tone. "My wife says I'm a cutie-pie too. That's why I listen to her."

Trouble is, I don't know who to listen to—my rules, the voice, George, or someone else.

Good thing Kingsley hands out the clues next, telling the teams that the first to complete the task and send in photographic proof wins that challenge.

On the count of three, the teams rip open the envelopes. I peer at the piece of paper, reading the words.

Everyone likes to leave his or her mark. It's a sign of the human condition to paint, scrawl, draw, or write your name on a wall. Indeed, graffiti is found all over this city, even in an Egyptian area, where the years don't always align, but where a signature arrived out of time.

Find it, take a photo with your team, then snap a picture outside demonstrating how you work together. Two-hour deadline. Fifty points.

18

LULU

We huddle. We confab. We study the clue, whispering it under our collective breaths. We speak with hushed voices, as if we're protecting something precious, and we try to figure out where this riddle might lead us.

And then, it crystallizes. Like the sun rising over the horizon, and all at once the sky is bright. "I know what it is."

I gather them close and tell my team members. Leo's smile is magnetic and proud. Noah thrusts a fist in the air, John Bender *Breakfast Club*–style.

Ginny squeezes my arm. "Girl power."

I point to the subway entrance. "Let's get on the nearest train."

My feet are ready to fly when Noah slices a hand through the air. "This is the wrong time of day for the subway. It'll take fifteen minutes, but we can snag an Uber like that, and be uptown in ten."

Noah whips out his cell phone, swipes his thumb

across it, and, like he's the fastest draw in the West, he calls an Uber. It's here in forty-five seconds.

"Impressive transportation skills," Ginny says.

"I have many impressive skills."

"Is that so?"

"That is indeed so. I can share them with you over dinner."

"We should have dinner to talk about your impressive skills?"

"We could have dinner to talk about other impressive things."

Ginny shakes her head, laughing as we head uptown, and I guess Noah's attempt to ask out Ginny hasn't quite hit the mark.

Along the way, I send a quick text to Cameron, who's still on the road working on more deals, and then to my new shop manager, who's been doing a bang-up job so far here in Manhattan. All is well, they report.

I breathe a sigh of relief and devote all my energy to riddling.

Ten minutes later, we arrive at our destination.

The desire to run is intense. It looks like we're the first team here, and we hoof it up the steps, taking them two by two into the Metropolitan Museum of Art. I don't see any other teams here as we grab our tickets, thrusting bills at the ticket taker because credit cards would take too long, and then we race-walk down the corridor like we're 1980s New Yorkers doing that speed-walking thing, elbows snapping at our sides, legs moving as quickly as they can.

Down the hall, we scurry past a sign for a Gustav

Klimt visiting exhibit in the other wing, then rush by the Tomb of Perneb, and after that a gilded coffin.

A temple stands tall and proud in the middle of the museum, and it takes my breath away. More than two thousand years old, it must have so many stories to tell.

"If walls could talk," I whisper as we reach the Temple of Dendur, seen in films like *When Harry Met Sally* and *Ocean's 8*. We hunt around, trying desperately to find the graffiti.

My heart beats faster, and I hope I haven't made a mistake by assuming this is the location from the clue. I don't know if there actually is any graffiti on this temple, but when I read the clue, I had a gut feeling.

As I turn the corner, scanning the walls, I gasp.

"Guys." I motion for them to come over. I point to a name and a year carved into the temple. *Leonardo 1820.*

Leo regards it with a curious *huh.* "Who do you think that is?"

"Your long-lost relative?" Noah chimes in.

I glance at Leo. "Now you know I want to find out."

Noah shakes a finger at me. "Now is not the time to satisfy your curiosity, Miss Diamond. We need to finish up the task because we're on track to be the first team to win today, and hopefully to beat everyone else by a long shot."

"My, my, someone is slightly competitive," Ginny remarks.

He shoots her an *isn't that obvious* look. "I have my reasons."

"What are they?"

He looks her over. "Everyone loves a winner."

Ah, there's more to his competitiveness than I'd thought. Noah is trying to win her heart by . . . winning.

Noah gathers us all in front of the temple, and we take a selfie, pointing to the graffiti. Our photograph is proof that we were here, and hopefully we're the first to reach our clue.

As we rush back outside to complete the last item in the task—a photo demonstrating teamwork—Leo nudges me. "What do you think that graffiti was all about? I saw on a placard that some European tourists left marks on the temple way back when this was still in Egypt."

"That's what I think it was. Graffiti, plain and simple."

"You don't think that guy was anyone special?"

"Everyone is someone special. But no, I don't think it means anything. Sometimes a cigar is just a cigar."

"And sometimes Leonardo from the early 1800s likes to leave his mark on temples?"

"Evidently." I smile at him, and he shoots an easy, lopsided one back at me.

Sometimes conversations are simple. Sometimes they're about what they're about.

They aren't about fear or worry or anything else. They aren't about whether someone is coming home late or drunk or has missed another day of work.

They are what they are.

Once we're on the front steps again, we toss around ideas for how to show teamwork, and we settle on an easy answer, but one that demonstrates it perfectly.

I take a deep, steadying breath. "Don't drop me."

Leo asks a tourist to take our picture.

On the middle step, on the count of three, my team-mates lift me over their heads. Leo's strong hands curve around my hips as he forms the foundation, holding me and lifting me higher, and higher still.

For a split second, I worry that I might fall, but then I talk back to my nervous mind because that's an ancient worry. I worried all the time with Tripp.

I worried he'd be late for a date. I worried he'd miss an appointment. Worried he'd miss payment on a bill.

My throat tightens as I recall the pain of losing my husband not to someone else but to some*thing* else. A potent, powerful siren that had Tripp in its grasp until his last days.

In our case, everything was about that something else. Everything was about addiction, dependency, denial.

Right now, I shove that all away.

This moment is a new moment. A beautiful morning. It's a day we can make our mark on.

So I leave graffiti on the air.

"Leonardo 1820," I call out, under a crystal-blue sky on the steps of the Metropolitan Museum of Art in Manhattan. I'm held by one person I know well and two people I'm getting to know. But I have no worries. They won't let me fall.

Knowing that, feeling it in my bones—I'm ebullient.

The tourist snaps the picture.

After Leo sets me down, Ginny sends in the picture, effectively recording our time to the finish line for this clue. "We don't have to return to the park for an hour or so."

Leo looks to me. "We have an hour and twenty-two minutes. What do you want to do, o riddle master?"

The answer comes into focus immediately. "I want to see the traveling Klimt exhibit. His paintings are here on loan from all over the world. Want to go with me?"

"Yes."

Ginny covers her eyes with her hand, squinting. "I'm hungry. I think I'll grab a pretzel."

Noah swivels around, jumping at the chance, it seems. "Pretzels are on me."

"But it's not a date."

"I know. It's only pretzels. I can buy the *only pretzels* though."

"But it's not a date for these *only pretzels*," she repeats.

"Someday it will be."

Ginny shakes her head, but she's smiling. "And that someday, it won't be pretzels."

Noah pumps a fist. "We'll start with a snack and work up to a *someday*."

As for me, I'm kind of hungry for a *someday* now.

19

LULU

Leo and I return to the museum, the leaderboard clearly on our side. As we walk toward the exhibit, I set my hand on his arm. I've always been a toucher, but Leo seems to like it, and honestly, I like touching him. It's comforting and familiar, but also unexpected, and in a good way. Glancing around, I say, "I love this place. My mom used to take me here all the time as a kid. Well, she took me everywhere. But this was one of our regular haunts."

"I remember you telling me that."

"You do?"

"Yeah, we've talked about everything over the years, it seems. All those late-night conversations."

"I loved our late-night conversations. Does that mean we have nothing new to say?"

He shakes his head. "It all feels new. Keep telling me stuff. What was your favorite part?"

I want to tell him stuff. Because it doesn't feel like we're playing the same record. It feels like we've tuned in to a familiar song, but on a whole new frequency.

As I reflect on his question, a memory flashes before me, bright and colorful. "The jewels. They had a display once of crown jewels. I loved them all, and I wanted to be a queen."

He chuckles. "Not a princess?"

"No way! I had much higher aspirations. Screw that whole damsel-in-distress, rescue-me stuff. I wanted to rule."

He shakes his head, amused. "Why am I not surprised?"

"Suits me, doesn't it?" I ask, laughing.

"To a T."

"And you? What did you like to do as a kid? Where did your parents take you? I seem to recall you showing me a photo of you and your brothers in front of the Liberty Bell."

"Naturally, we pretended we cracked it. And yeah, growing up in Philly, it was all history, Founding Fathers, and the Declaration of Independence. Our parents always took us to those historic sites. It was more fun than I expected, but I think it also gave me a healthy appreciation for the past."

I pause when he says that, taking a peek into his dark-brown eyes, searching for something. Something that worries me. *The past.* "Do you have that? A healthy appreciation for the past?"

"Yes." His answer is swift and certain, bursting with meaning.

I don't know if he means the historical past, our past, or something else. Maybe his own past with Tripp.

But when we reach the exhibit hall and my eyes land on a golden painting, I stop wondering about the days that came before because I'm transfixed by what's in front of me, visiting from its regular home in Vienna. Gustav Klimt's most famous work: *The Kiss*. The colors and the mosaic-like assembly of shades of jewels are mesmerizing.

The look on the woman's face draws me in as the man kisses her cheek. Her beauty is haunting. Her want is palpable. My arms seem to reach forward of their own accord. "Want."

He laughs. "For you, Lulu, I'll get it. I'll buy you a Klimt."

I shake my head, whispering reverently, "No. I want that kiss."

He turns to me, his brow knitted, his voice curious and a little unsure. "You do?"

"I want that. I feel so greedy, but yes, I do. I want *that*. I want a kiss like that." I'm taking a dangerous step here. I'm toying with something terribly risky. But this admission feels so necessary. This painting is doing things to me. Things that only chocolate has done. It stirs up so much longing.

"Have you had a kiss like that?" He looks as if it pains him to ask the question.

I want to answer, but I don't want to besmirch Tripp's memory, even though I'm not his widow. I'm his ex-wife. I left him because he loved his mistress more than me. But I don't want to compare his kisses. They're over.

An invisible thread pulls me closer to Leo. "It doesn't matter. It doesn't matter if I've had it."

His eyes hold mine, never wavering. I don't know what's happening with us. But I want this moment, wholly. I want it to unfurl like a red carpet. I'm eager to find out where it leads.

I want to be like Leonardo from 1820—to make a mark on history. On my history. And I want Leo, circa 2019.

I move even closer, not caring about the people at the museum admiring the painting. They are a static haze to me. Leo's as clear as the art. "I want that kiss."

"Then you should have it." His voice is gravelly, rough. It's strewn with hidden meaning, and I can read the clues.

We both want whatever this strange new thing is that's brewing between us.

We want it, even if we're afraid of it.

An inexorable pull tugs us closer together, like a magnet seeking its opposite. "That painting. Maybe it's kismet."

"You think so?" Another step.

"Maybe it's poetry."

He shakes his head, but he's smiling. "You and your poetry."

"What about you? What do you want?"

He licks his lips. "The same."

In front of the Klimt, in front of the crowd, Leo lifts his hand, curls it around the back of my head, and brings me close.

My breath stutters. Electricity shoots through my body. My feet barely touch the ground as he lowers his head and brushes a chaste kiss.

On my cheek.

That's not fair.

That's not what I want.

But even so, my body tingles all over. All from a kiss on my cheek.

And that kiss makes me want his lips.

I raise my face, cup his jaw, and make the chaste kiss not so chaste, after all.

He takes the baton and runs with it.

He kisses me tenderly, brushing his mouth over mine in a gentle exploration, like he's been dying to get to know my lips, but like he can take his time with them too.

Like he can take all the time in the world.

His kiss is full of longing as his lips sweep over mine, visiting the corners, traveling across the bow of them. Visiting everywhere.

I'm buzzing, my entire body humming like the start of a song—a song that'll build in seconds. As he takes his time,

the desire in me roars well past the speed limit. I break with desire.

It snaps me in two, and the hungry, ravenous half of me wins. My hand is on his face, so I bring him closer and crush my lips to his. I devour his mouth, taking him like he's mine, like he belongs to me.

He groans roughly, and it sounds both painful and intoxicating. *I'm* intoxicated as he deepens the kiss, his lips searching mine, finding me. Finding a new us. The kiss is his again as he draws me tight and consumes me.

We kiss like we're discovering a new land. Like we're leaving our mark on this moment. And we are. Because this is the record I want from today.

I don't need photographic proof to know it happened.

My mind is taking snapshots for me to look at later.

A new tour group shuffles into the room, and we break the kiss, looking at each other like *wow*.

But we also need to leave. We exit the museum through the gift shop, where Leo buys me a postcard of *The Kiss* then signs it.

Leo 2019. The Met. Klimt Exhibit.

In my mind, I add one more line.

First kiss.

* * *

Along with Ginny and Noah, we return to the starting place for the hunt, where the Heavenly Four, as we've dubbed ourselves, are in first place on the first day.

Then we're back at the office, working on chocolate and business deals.

As I leave for my shop, ready to dive into my recipes for the afternoon, I spot Leo heading into a meeting.

He doesn't see me.

He doesn't even look like he's here.

He's somewhere else, and I know that look.

He's lost in the past.

And I want both to know what he's thinking of and to erase our whole history.

20

LEO

Two and a half years ago

Only one person knew.

That was Dean, and he was a vault.

I planned to take my feelings for her to the grave, especially since they were ancient history. Hell, they were ancient history well before Lulu asked me to help convince Tripp to go to rehab.

And because those feelings were no longer a fact of my daily existence, I intended to keep them locked in a safe with an unbreakable combination, even when Tripp stumbled up the steps to my apartment late one night, unshaven, reeking of tequila and beer.

"Just promise me one thing," he said. Lulu had left him earlier that year, a few weeks after he'd earned himself a swift exodus from rehab for cheating on the program with Jose Cuervo. I suspected he and Jose had been cozying up tonight too.

"What's that?" I brewed a pot of coffee. It would do nothing for him. I knew that. It was an old wives' tale. Nothing makes you un-drunk but time and stopping. But I made the coffee anyway.

He slumped against the kitchen doorway. "Promise me—that when you finally go for it with her, you'll tell me first."

A steel rod plunged through my spine. I stood straighter, my mind clanging, blood rushing between my ears. My head felt like a gong had rung inside it. How the hell did he know? I was iron. I was inscrutable.

"With Amy?" I tossed out, since I'd just met a great gal named Amy and was thinking about asking her out. *Please, God, let him be talking about Amy.*

He cracked up, scrubbing a hand over his chin. "Seriously?"

"Seriously, what?" I was skilled in the practice of stoicism. I had a poker face to rival an entire Texas Hold'em tournament.

"Leo, you're my best friend. You're like a brother to me. You think I don't know?"

"Don't know what?" I poured the boiling water, and I'd never been so grateful for a distraction.

He stepped into the kitchen, grabbing at the counter to steady himself.

"How much did you drink tonight?"

He waved a hand dismissively. "Hardly anything. I'm tough. I'm like that chick in *Raiders of the Lost Ark*. She can drink those big-ass dudes under the table. What's her name?"

"Marion. Her name is Marion." I thrust a steaming mug at him, the words on the cup mocking me because it was a gift from *her*—*But first, coffee*. Simple, heartfelt, and true.

"Marion! That's it."

It was as if I'd given him the key to a treasure chest, and I'd hoped and prayed the distraction would work. "Drink your coffee. There's a blanket on the couch. You can crash here."

He downed a hearty gulp then slapped the mug on the counter with a clatter. Brown liquid spilled over the side. "Sorry. I'm sorry."

"It's okay. It's just coffee."

"It's not. It's your favorite thing."

"We are not getting sentimental over coffee or counters."

"But what about Lulu?"

"What about her?"

He sighed, staring at me. "Leo. I figured it out a year ago. Stop avoiding me. I know."

"Know what?" My whole delicate balancing act threatened to topple.

"I know you're in love with Lulu. I realized it in rehab."

Slice me open with a serrated knife. "You're ridiculous."

"It was all crystal clear. You know what else was crystal clear?" He patted my chest, his eyes forlorn but resolute at the same time. "You're the better man. You're the man she should have been with."

My gut twisted for fifty-million reasons. "Fuck off."

"No, I mean it. You have your shit together. I'm a mess."

"You could get your act together if you wanted."

That's what irked me the most. Help was his alone to get.

He shrugged. "Maybe. But listen, will you? Tell me first?"

My jaw ticked angrily. I wanted to shout *enough!* But after all this time, after all these years, I wasn't giving an inch, not after all he'd done, and all he'd never done. "You're ridiculous. I'm not in love with her."

"Just promise me."

I wasn't letting him win this. He was drunk. I was sober. I had the upper hand of clarity, and I would wield it. I also had the truth on my side. "There's nothing to promise you because I'm not in love with her."

It was the truth, the whole truth, and nothing but.

He was a dog with a bone. "Promise me you'll give me a heads-up before you go for it."

I poured some coffee and took a drink, hiding behind the mug. "This is an insane conversation, and it needs to end."

When he crashed on the couch a few minutes later, he didn't let go. His voice was threadbare. "Promise me."

"Tripp."

"Just promise."

"There's nothing to promise."

He sat up. I was parked in the chair. He grabbed my face sloppily. "Fucking promise."

I wanted to get away from him. Desperately. I let him win that battle. "Whatever. Yes. If it gets you to go to sleep."

He smiled. "I'll sleep like a baby."

He curled to his side.

We never spoke of that night again.

21

LEO

Present Day

Running doesn't work.

Gorging on South American history doesn't work.

Furniture stripping doesn't work.

My mind is a depot, and two trains keep slamming into each other.

One is the kiss.

The other is a conversation with my dead best friend.

The two can't coexist.

And I can't talk to him again. I can't ask him for permission. I can't honor a promise I made late one night at my apartment a few months before he died, a promise I veiled as a simple excuse to get him to shut up. I can't honor it because he took that away from me too, the night he got behind the wheel after too much to drink, drove too fast, and crashed his car into a tree.

Fucking tree.

Fucking Tripp.

That was five days after we'd gone to dinner at a hot new restaurant he'd been raving about. The Red Door. He'd gotten us into The Red Door, and the fucker hadn't even been drinking that night. He had iced tea, and he gave me hope.

Hope that he was finally turning the corner.

Five days later, he was gone.

Tonight, I pace through my apartment, wishing I could get in a cab uptown, bang my fist on the door of his pad, and tell him I'm taking her out, and that's that, then go to the batting cage the next day with him and laugh about whatever had cracked us up that week at work.

Like we used to.

There's so much we used to do that we'll never do again.

And I've dealt with all of it. I've mourned him, missed him, and moved on.

But that promise—that stupid promise—hangs over me.

He can't grant me a thing anymore, and I don't know that Lulu can either, but at least I can see her, talk to her.

That's a choice I do have.

I head downtown, straight for Lulu's home, texting her that I'm on the way.

She buzzes me in. Tension coils in me as I walk up the steps slowly, as if each successive footfall will sort out the mayhem in my mind.

It's a mess in there.

More than ten years after I met her, I finally kissed the woman I've loved.

The woman I can't get out of my head.

She's back in full force, the deed to my heart in her hand, and I need to know what she's going to do with it.

I reach her floor, scanning for 3B. I locate it instantly when I spot a neon-pink Christmas stocking hanging from a door. In felt-tip pen on the cuff are the words "Feel free to drop any assorted packages, bills, or winning lottery tickets here."

I let myself imagine her apartment. What does a Lulu-only place look like? Colorful, vibrant, teeming with all the things?

I knock, and she opens the door right away, dropping into her best Mae West impression. "Why don't you come up sometime and see me?" She takes a beat. "Oh, you're already here. Come in."

"Why, thank you very much," I say, Cary Granting it back to her.

She's more knock 'em dead than any silver-screen stunner. More than Mae West, Rita Hayworth, and Marilyn herself, even in blue leggings that stop below her knees and a pale-yellow T-shirt that falls off her shoulder.

I step inside, entering a kaleidoscope. A ruby-red fleece blanket is draped across a purple couch. Pillows are piled high on the ends of that sofa, towering and teetering like Jenga blocks. Picture frames stand proudly on nearly every surface—images of Lulu and her mom laughing at a bookstore, Lulu and her colleague Cameron at their first shop, Lulu and

Mariana on the beach. I can't help it—I scan for one of Lulu and Tripp, but find none.

An unexpected dose of delight zips through me. This discovery makes me happier than it should, so I do my best to wipe that cocky smile off my face as I peer around, noticing magazines stacked across a small table and books rising sky-high on a shelf.

Lulu is not a neat freak. Lulu is like a suitcase that you sit on to try to close, but bright emerald-green scarves poke out the corners, a fuchsia-pink heel sticks out one side, and a polka-dotted dress spills from the zipper.

Everything is a little bit messy and wild.

In the kitchen, a mint-green KitchenAid mixer takes center stage. A steel canister holds utensils and whisks, and the counter is shiny and spotless. An open pack of chocolate tells me she's already been experimenting with concoctions this evening. The scents of vanilla and almond tell me she's made something delicious.

"The whole place—it's very you. Like you stamped it with an ink pad."

She shuts the door. "Lulu's lair. Enter at your own risk."

I laugh. "I'll consider myself warned."

"But will you heed the warning? After all, you're here." She raises her chin and looks at me with challenge in her eyes.

"I'm here. I suppose that means I'm not entirely risk averse."

A smile tries to sneak across her lips, but she seems

to tuck it away. "So . . ." She exhales, waiting. She's waiting for me.

Of course she is.

It's my move.

She served first earlier today.

I drum my fingers across the foyer table. "What are we doing?"

"Right now? Talking."

"You know what I mean."

She shrugs, looking as helpless as I feel. "I don't know."

"I mean, are we on the way to dating or something?" That's the strangest thing to say. How can I begin to conceive of Lulu and me dating? What would a date look like? We've done so many things together already.

"Do you want to date?" she asks.

"Do you?"

We're two racquetball players, volleying, neither one wanting to cede.

She heads to the kitchen, grabs a bottle of sparkling water from the fridge, and pours two glasses, then stops. "Do you want wine instead?" But she answers her own question before I can. "I'm not having any."

I wave it off. "I'm good."

And it's refreshing. To take it or leave it. We can both walk away from wine.

She hands me a glass, and I drink. She drinks too.

When I set it down, I try again. "What do you want, Lulu?"

"I want a lot of things. I want us to date and go out and kiss like the world is ending. I want us to laugh and run on the beach and chase the moon."

God, they sound like all my dreams, but I can hear the *but* coming. There will always be one with the two of us.

She takes another sip. "But it's foolish, right? How could it be anything but foolish if we were together? My life was mostly a mess for the last decade," she says softly, desperately. "I lost out on so many opportunities and chances. I finally have one. I don't want to risk it."

I swallow roughly. I don't want her to risk her chances either. "We need to make it through this partnership. Whatever is happening between the two of us was probably all stirred up stuff from the past."

She looks at me quizzically. "The past? What would be stirred up from the past?"

I realize my mistake, and I backpedal, since I don't want her to know how long I've wanted to kiss her. "I meant since we've known each other so long. Been through so much. Been friends and all that stuff."

"I hear you, but just so you know, there was nothing stirred up from the past today for me. That was all present-day stuff. I never saw you that way in the past. You're not offended, are you?"

I breathe a huge sigh of relief for two reasons. Because she isn't on to me, and because I don't want her to have felt a thing for me when she was with him.

"I'm not offended at all."

She takes a drink of water then sets down the glass. "Are we still friends?"

I laugh. "You're going to have to try a lot harder for us to be un-friends."

She smiles. "Good. I'm famished. Do you want dinner?"

"I won't turn you down."

She grabs items from the fridge then sets to work. Lulu slices the tops off small green peppers, tosses them into a skillet sizzling with olive oil, and sautés them with some salt and pepper. The pan sizzles, and she stirs.

She scoops up a pepper onto a spatula and brandishes it. Wiggling an eyebrow, she asks, "Can you handle the heat?"

That question feels like the doublest of double entendres. "Bring. It. On."

"You're so tough."

"You don't know the half of it." If she knew the armor I had wielded over the years, she'd think I was made of metal.

She blows on the pepper then dangles it in front of me. "Catch it?"

"Do it."

She tosses over a pepper.

I'm a frog. I stick out my tongue and catch it. It's hot, but I've never had trouble handling spice.

I bite into the pepper, and it nearly scalds my tongue, but I crunch away, chewing with as much of a smile as I can muster, even as the green goodie torches my mouth. She watches me, appreciation etched into those eyes.

"Impressed?" I want to impress her. Hell, if we were in the 1950s, I'd be the guy on the beach, flexing his biceps for the girl.

"Don't you know? Nearly everything you do impresses me."

And the bicep curls worked.

Nice job, self.

She stretches for a cupboard, reaching to grab an open bag of popcorn. She dips her hand inside, then backhands a kernel my way. I bend, catching that on my tongue too. "Now that is doubly impressive. In fact, I might need to enter you in a competition at SeaWorld."

"*Arf, arf,*" I say, imitating a seal.

"Speaking of sea creatures, I have on my dolphin panties today."

"Seriously?"

"Want to see?"

What the hell? The woman just said we need to stay in the friend zone, and now she's offering to show me her panties. Can we say *women are confusing*?

"Is that a trick question? Are you testing me?"

She laughs. "What's the answer?"

I move closer. "I always want to see your underwear. So don't ask a silly question again."

"What if I want to see your underwear?"

"You're like an open flame, Lulu."

She laughs. "I know. Sorry. Grab me the green beans?"

We shift gears, and I help her as she stir-fries green beans, sautés chicken, plates it all, and sets the table. It's just us and this delicious spread she's whipped up— and the big elephant in the room.

Our kiss.

We only discussed if it should happen again, not how much we want it to. Her words from earlier echo —*I want us to date and go out and kiss like the world is ending.*

The elephant is trundling across her apartment,

rattling the pictures on the walls. We eat, and the tension spreads across my shoulders. This tiptoeing won't do. We aren't some guy and girl who met at a bar. We aren't coworkers who've known each other for a year and finally gave in to the wild flirtation we've had in the elevator. We are people who talk. We use our words.

After we finish, I say, "We should really talk about the elephant."

"It was a particularly wonderful elephant."

That's the oddest compliment I've ever received for a kiss, but I love it.

"It was." I replay that kiss for the five thousandth time today. I stare at her lips, remembering how they felt against mine.

"You're looking at my mouth," she whispers.

A weight slides off my shoulder and thuds to the ground. It feels like freedom. I can look at Lulu and speak some of the truth. "Your mouth is quite lush. Soft. Inviting."

She shivers, swaths of her curly hair falling across half of her face, curtaining her green eye. I reach an arm across and tuck the curls behind her ear as best I can. I want to see into those eyes. I want to read them. "Lulu, what are we doing?"

She stares up at me from underneath those long lashes. "Remembering earlier today?"

"It was mind-blowing."

"Was it really that way for you?" There's a vulnerability in her tone, as if she doesn't quite believe it could have been spectacular for me.

She has no idea that it was everything I've ever

wanted and a thousand times more. Because it was real. Because it happened now.

Between only the two of us.

Because it didn't come when we were helping Tripp or grieving Tripp.

It came from living.

I circle back to her question then give her my answer. "It *was* that way. It was the only way."

"What happens next?"

That's the question. It keeps hanging in the air, and it's going to demand a thorough dissection. Saying *How could it be anything but foolish if we were together?* isn't enough of an answer.

Her foot slides up my leg. I arch a brow. "Lulu, are you playing footsie with me?"

"What's wrong with that?" She looks ridiculously innocent.

"That's not friendly."

"It's a foot, Leo."

"Your foot is not friendly."

"Oh, come on. You're not turned on by my foot, are you?"

"No."

She gives me a sly stare. "Are you sure?" She rubs her foot closer to my crotch. "Because it feels like you might be."

She is dangerously near my erection, and yes, I am indeed turned on by her foot. Big surprise. This woman has done it for me for years. "Lulu . . ."

"Sorry, I thought maybe you had a banana in your pocket."

I laugh. "You're not helping matters."

I reach under the table, grab her foot, and run my hand over it, kneading the sole. She groans, and it sounds sensual, like she's a woman who loves to indulge—in food, in pleasures, in riches of the senses. She leans her head back, her long, glorious neck exposed as she closes her eyes. I want to learn if the coconut that I've smelled on her for ages is there when I kiss the column of her neck, the hollow of her throat. I knead harder into her foot.

"Don't do that. It'll make me moan and groan."

"You're already groaning. You're already killing me."

She opens her eyes. "I can't help it. You have strong hands, and they feel good on my feet."

She sits up straighter and sets her hands on the table. I let go of her foot.

"Leo, I don't think I realized how attractive you were before, and I'm glad I didn't. But it's all hitting me at once. And right now, I kind of want to jump you. I want to throw the plates to the ground, crawl across the table, and straddle you. I want to grind against you and kiss you all over and do all sorts of very bad things to you."

I sit stiller than a statue, absorbing the sizzle of those words.

If I ever thought my resistance was going to be tested, this is the moment, and whatever shred I possess is fraying at the seams. "There's literally nothing I want more."

She stares at me with heat in her eyes.

It's nearly enough to melt the last thread of resistance.

But her next words halt me in my tracks. "But I have

plans, and I have a chance to finally focus on them. I don't want to lose my focus. That would be foolish. Don't you think?"

And there it is—the reluctance.

I have enough of my own to feed an army. I can't take on the burden of hers too. I can't give in to all this heat if it's seasoned with both our reluctant lusts.

"Maybe I should go before we do something foolish."

I wait for her to echo me, as I know she will.

She swallows and breathes out harshly, repeating my assessment. "Yes. You probably should."

Somehow, I find the will to stand, but I can't locate the strength to leave just yet. "Do you want me to clean up?"

She squeezes her eyes shut. "No. You should probably leave."

That's exactly what I do.

22

LEO

That was one of the hardest things I've ever done.

Like shit-they-do-in-the-movies tough.

It was on the same level as hacking into Las Vegas's traffic system in five seconds, pulling someone up from quicksand using only one arm, or jumping through a glass window. I bet if I tried that last one, I'd just bounce back with a loud thump.

But I can't bounce back, and I don't have a clue how to move forward.

In the morning, I rise before dawn, hoping to run off this pandemonium of thoughts and banging cymbals in my head.

I circle the reservoir, trying to drain my brain of last night, of Lulu, of all the things I want to say to her.

As I near the end of my run, a familiar set of footsteps roars by.

Squeals.

Stops.

"Yo!" It's Noah. "Hey, slowpoke."

"Hey, cheetah."

"I'm breaking through all my land speed records. Also, I owe you a big, huge, massive thank you. I knew you were the man."

"What are you thanking me for?"

"Your brilliant, genius, insanely awesome advice to ask out Ginny."

I arch a brow. "She said yes?"

"She let me buy her pretzels. And they were the best pretzels under the sun. It's a start, right? Gotta start somewhere."

That is true.

That is very true.

In fact, maybe that's my new rule to live by.

Start somewhere.

"Whatever it takes to get the girl, right?" he adds with a wave as he takes off to the other side of the world, flying on those Mercury legs.

Taking action.

Making a start.

And the commotion in my head clears instantly.

I don't need to take a back seat this time.

After a little googling upon my return home, I know what I want to say to the woman I was in love with for the better part of a decade.

You have to start somewhere.

23

LULU

Kickboxing with my friends always clears my head. I've never been a solo exerciser. I like the company and the chatter. I like the girl power, and I instruct Mariana not to mention men at all.

She gives a thumbs-up. "Man-diet morning. Got it. I vow to only discuss frivolous things to keep your mind off whatever man is driving you crazy."

"You're a true friend."

At six in the morning, Mariana and I sweat our way through a killer class that elevates my heart rate to skyscraper levels. We speak in our exercise shorthand, the cardio reducing us to quick, bullet-like sentences as I tell her briefly about Heavenly, how the new line has started to come together over the last few weeks, the flavors I'm trying, as well as the hunt.

When we hit the cool-down phase, I can breathe and talk more normally. "Plus, business at the shop is strong. I can't really complain about anything, so, ya know, I won't," I say as I stretch.

"Considering my newest client just paid me an obscene retainer, I won't complain either. But I did donate ten percent of it to Little Friends, the local animal rescue."

"Whoa. Did they erect a statue of you in front of the shelter? Because for ten percent, they should."

Mariana laughs. "Nope. But that's my goal. Someday, somewhere, I'd like a statue erected. Mostly because statues are one of the few times you can say 'erect' without getting the side-eye."

I give her the side-eye. "I think that's one of those words that always deserves a side-eye."

She lowers her voice to a whisper. "Yes, it does. Also, I won the bet."

"What bet?"

"I bet Cameron that you'd try to wear the pantsuit. He bet you wouldn't even take it from my house. I know you so well."

I jam my elbow into her side.

"Ouch."

"You set me up!"

"I know, but you asking me for a suit was the most absurd thing you've ever done, and you've done some absurd things."

"Like what? Name one."

"Like the time you wanted to attend a circus class."

"I still want to learn to juggle."

That sends us down a rabbit hole discussion of circus skills we'd most want to possess—she picks fire-eating and I choose trapeze.

But in the end, Mariana tells me she's glad I chose

chocolate. "You're doing exactly what you're supposed to be doing."

"Why do you say that?"

"Because of your sweet caramel center," she says with a wink.

"What's yours made of?"

"Steel and vitriol."

"Have I mentioned I never want to go up against you in a court of law?"

* * *

When our class is over and we've made plans to do it again a few days later, my head is officially clear.

Clear of that kiss.

Clear of last night.

Clear of this bizarre new phase in my life where I'm suddenly wildly attracted to Leo Hennessy.

He's always been interesting, kind, and clever.

He's always been smart and easy to talk to.

And he's definitely always been handsome. I'm not blind, and I wasn't before Lasik either. I know he's hot, just like I know Chris Hemsworth could swindle the panties off any woman, but I don't want to jump him. Wait, that's not true. Chris Hemsworth is everyone's hall pass.

Be that as it may, I never thought of Leo in a romantic way.

My eyes were laser-focused on Tripp, my heart belonging 100 percent to the man I married.

Given how it ended, given how it all spiraled downhill, do I regret my choice to love him?

No.

I learned resilience from my marriage. I learned I wasn't responsible for other people's choices. I discovered that I couldn't fix another person, no matter how hard I tried.

Tripp is my past. Tripp is behind me. I've made peace with my marriage, with what it was and what it was not. That's why I don't harbor any guilt over Leo.

This issue is different.

It's how he fits into my life.

As I return to my apartment and shower, I contemplate *if* he fits into my life now that I have room to breathe, to plan, and to grow my business. Do I fling all those ingredients to the floor to indulge in a newfound lust?

But this isn't lust.

It's so much more.

Leo is the guy who shows up.

Leo is the guy who will be there.

The recipe of feelings plus Leo equals the real deal.

The trouble is timing.

I'm finally free to live my life on my terms, and those terms include my partnership with his company.

As I rinse off, step out of the shower, and grab a towel, I don't know that I can fit the real deal in my life at this moment.

A heavy blanket of sadness falls over me. But along with that sadness comes something new.

Determination.

I'm on the other side. I'm rebuilding and remaking my life. I love the freedom from madness. I love the opportunities unfurling before me.

I love my choices.

And I need to behave like I have them. I text the smartest person I know.

Lulu: What exactly did you mean when you said he had years in his eyes?

Mom: It feels like there's a different question in there than the one you're asking, so I'll ask it. Why are you asking me this question?

Lulu: I shouldn't be surprised that you answered a question with a question.

Mom: However else would I answer it? :)

Lulu: So. Years. Explain.

Mom: I said he had years in his eyes because he looks at you in a way that's different from how a man looks at a woman he's simply attracted to.

I stare at the text message, trying to decode it. But it's almost too much, the notion she's presenting. I can't conceive of years. All I know is he kissed me like a man possessed. But what possessed him?

The idea of years is inconceivable. He's dated other women. He was engaged, for crying out loud. He can't possibly have wanted me for years, so I decide that he hasn't, and I deal with only the here and now.

And that mesmerizing kiss.

Lulu: We kissed yesterday.

Mom: WAY TO BURY THE LEDE!

Lulu: I was teeing you up. :)

Mom: This is huge!

Lulu: Is it?

Mom: I presume you don't go around kissing random men for kicks?

Lulu: I haven't kissed anyone in years. I haven't dated anyone since my marriage ended. You know that. So, what happens next?

Mom: What does your heart say? What do you want? Was it just a random kiss? Or was it a kiss that leads to more late-night bookstore visits and dinners with your mother?

My face flushes as I read the last lines, like I've been busted.

And I have.

The kiss won't lead to late-night bookstore visits and dinners with my mom, because late-night bookstore visits and dinners with my mom were what led to the kiss.

So were museum visits.

And nights out at The Pub.

And text messages.

And *time*. Spending time with Leo.

That's the cause, and the kiss was the effect.

I want more of the effect. So much more.

As I reflect back on the last month, I can see with my twenty-twenty vision that we've been spinning toward that kiss since I bumped into a chocolate fountain and found myself on top of him. I recall every second of the kiss, reliving the tingles that swept over me, the hum under my skin, the joy that seemed to radiate in my bones. The joy of possibility. Of a new kind of connection.

But I'm not entirely sure how to sum all that up to fit into one category of kissing. Still, I try my best when I write back to her.

Lulu: Would you think I was a complete cheeseball if I told you it was magical?

Mom: I'd think you were the daughter I raised. There are no better kisses than the kind that are magical. The kind that make your toes tingle.

Lulu: That's exactly the kind we had. But I feel like I'd be stupid to pursue anything, given that I'm contracted with his company. I shouldn't mess around with this chance in my career. Don't you think?

Mom: I think your career is a precious thing and ought to be handled with care.

Lulu: So it's settled. I choose chocolate over kisses?

Mom: Is that the choice?

Lulu: I thought that's what you were saying.

Mom: I'm not going to tell you what to do. The heart wants what the heart wants.

Lulu: And you always taught me both to listen to mine and not be fooled by it.

Mom: I did, because there is no organ more susceptible to trickery, subterfuge, or sabotage than the heart. Embrace it, treat it as something precious, and be very wary of it.

I tuck the phone away in my purse. I am so very wary of hearts.

24

LULU

Today's starting point?

Washington Square Park.

As I walk under the arch, I pass three team members from Frodo's as they engage in tree poses and practice mantras.

"I visualize myself on a beach, soaking in the warm rays."

"I see myself walking along the streets of Paris."

"I'm on a golf course, nailing a hole in one."

Damn, the prospect of winning a vacation is some kind of powerful lure.

Granted, I have nothing against tropical beaches or fabulous foreign cities, but I've never been a give-me-vacation-or-give-me-death kind of girl.

There are other things I want though.

Maybe I ought to practice visualizing what I want.

I'm kissing Leo again. I'm tackling him, rolling around with him, and taking him home. He's sliding inside me, kissing my neck, and making me—

SCREECH.

What the hell?

When did I become the dirtiest bird when it came to that man?

When you mauled him in front of a Klimt, you dodo.

Oh, well, that would do it.

I had mega sex dreams about Leo last night. They were utterly delicious, and I regret nothing.

Not a damn thing.

A man clears his throat, and I glance in the direction of the scoffer. The Finger-Licking-Good Guy. He nods at the collection of Frodo employees, rolling his eyes. "You know where I see myself?"

"Where's that?"

The man sighs majestically and spreads his arms. "In my La-Z-Boy, watching a game."

I give him a thumbs-up. "Squad goals," I say, using Leo's words from the chocolate show.

His brow knits. "Hey, listen. You're the lady who fell in the fountain, aren't you?"

"Just call me Chocolate-Covered Lulu."

"Listen, sorry about that. I was the one running the booth that day, and I couldn't believe that happened."

I flash back to the fountain incident. This affable fellow hardly seems like the guy who accused Leo of rolling around in his fountain, but indeed he is. "You know what they say. Chocolate fountain incidents are a little unbelievable. Did you ever get the tipper you were looking for?"

"Alas, I didn't catch the scofflaw."

"Dammit," I say. "We could try to track him down. Put up a wanted poster perhaps?"

"Oh, he's already on the FBI's Ten Most Wanted. The search will go on."

"Never give up. Never surrender."

He laughs then smiles again. "So, about that day. I was kind of frenzied and frustrated because of some stuff going on at home with the babies—"

"Babies? As in multiple?"

"The wife had triplets six months ago."

My eyes bulge. "I can't imagine. No wonder she wants you to have time off. But is everything okay with them? How are they doing? What sort of stuff is going on? Do you need more caffeine?"

"I always need more caffeine. My little Helena is colicky. She's been crying like crazy, and Emma, that's my wife—she's having a hard time with it."

"I have to imagine she is." Then I smile because . . . *babies*. There are definitely stars in my eyes. "Can I see pictures?"

A surprised smile comes my way. "Yeah. Are you sure?"

"Hello?! Show me the trio!"

After grabbing his phone from his pocket, he clicks on a folder then shows me a picture of three chubby-cheeked redheads. My heart turns to mush, and I coo at the photos. "I love them."

"That's how I felt when I met them too."

"More, more. Show me more."

The man flips through his camera roll, and I squeal at nearly every adorable shot of the chunks of love, including one of the girls sitting upright in Daddy's La-Z-Boy.

When we're through, I'm a soft teddy bear. "This is

the best."

"Anyway, that's why I was so flustered that day about the fountain— "

"Don't think twice about it. We are all good. I landed a job out of it."

And landed on top of a man who tastes better than a truffle and melts my insides like chocolate, and now I'm falling for him in a delicious way. So, really, I suppose it's fitting I fell into a fountain.

"No kidding?"

I square my shoulders. "I'm Lulu Diamond. I'm making chocolate for Heavenly for its Rising Star line."

He offers a fist for knocking. "George Day. Rock on, chocolate-covered chocolatier."

"Rock on, Triple Latte Daddy."

I say goodbye and continue my trek across the park to my team.

As Leo comes into view, I smile from the inside out. Maybe the baby pictures primed me, but I'm grinning like a bit of a fool. When he smiles back, I upgrade myself to beaming. Full wattage–style.

Leo gestures to the cup of coffee in his hand. *But first, coffee*, he mouths then adds, *for you*.

My squishy heart softens more.

He strides over, a little grin tugging at his lips like we have a secret. The secret is we want to jump each other.

But we want so much more too.

And we can't quite have it.

Instead, we have . . . coffee.

He hands me a cup. "With cream, as you like it."

"Life is too short to drink coffee without cream."

"Gotta have standards."

"Also, thank you." It's a little thing, but it's also a wonderful thing. And I like the little things in life. I take a sip, and the drink is mixed perfectly, and I tell him as much.

"One of my talents—remembering how you like your coffee." He lowers his voice. "Listen, about last night."

The night I practically flung myself at him. "Don't worry about it."

"I'm not worried, Lulu."

"Then what is it?"

Nerves thrum through me. His words move like stop-and-start traffic. "Last night . . . you . . . the things you said. I think my brain was a pinball game."

The nerves tighten like a valve. "Did you beat the game?"

"No. I don't know how it plays out."

"I don't either."

"I know it's foolish, but fuck, you're in my head, Lulu. I have this for you." He reaches into his back pocket and takes out a small postcard. "I looked this up this morning online. I thought you would like it. I picked up some cardstock and printed it out."

My breath catches as I turn the card over, and something so pedestrian occurs to me—he bought cardstock to print this. Now, this is a big thing. This is a thoughtful thing. It requires planning and foresight. It's like shopping for a gourmet dinner, concocting a wonderful meal, and serving it with the perfect garnish.

And it's an even bigger thing when I see what he's printed.

An image of Man Ray's photo dubbed *The Kiss*, a close-up shot of a couple's lips almost meeting. The thunder before the lightning strikes.

A pinwheel spins inside me, shooting off colors and sparks. I turn the card over, but he clasps his hand over mine. "Read it later."

I bat my eyelashes. "Please? Now?"

He laughs. "So impatient."

"I want to read it." My voice betrays me, and I don't care. I am desperate to know what he wrote.

He relents. "You're irresistible. Next time, I'll get you the Chagall."

"I love Chagall's kissing painting."

"Of course you do."

Smiling with utter delight at my accomplishment—convincing him—I turn it over and read his words.

I can't stop thinking about you.

My heart glows. My blood runs neon. I'm a firework shooting high into the summer sky.

I meet his eyes. They're a warm chocolate brown, and they're sketched with tenderness and desire.

Something else is stamped in them too. *Hope.*

This card, these words—they don't change the reality of him, me, and my personal goal to focus on building a business. But even so, I'd be a fool of another kind if I let this moment pass me by. "It's the same for me."

In some other world, some other place, we'd fall into the close-up shot of an almost-kiss. And then we'd become *The Kiss*.

In this world, sneakers slap the pavement, and I straighten instantly.

"What's the same for you?"

It's Noah, splashing cold water on us as he runs closer in running shorts, showing off his golden skin.

"Are you dressed for a run?" I ask, doing my best one-eighty.

"You know that adage about dressing for the job you want? I want us to be first place at the end of today, so I'm dressing like Usain Bolt."

Leo lifts an appreciative brow. "Is this your second run of the day?"

"Hell, yeah. One wasn't enough. After I left you in the dust and went home, I had a ton of energy, so I ran down here. And I came up with awesome ideas as I ran this morning. Speaking of, I had this killer new idea for sales. Want to hear it? We have a few minutes before we start."

Leo nods and turns to me, mouthing *later*.

I motion that I'll join them in a few, then I take a sip of my coffee, fueling up.

* * *

"Hey, Lulu!"

I turn in the direction of the voice and I see the white-blonde RaeLynn striding over to me.

"Hi, RaeLynn."

"I was hoping to catch up with you. I've been reading about your chocolates, and everything I've seen on blogs about you is tremendous. You were picked as one of BuzzFeed's Top Five Chocolatiers to watch."

"Thank you. I was honored to be named."

"I know you're working with Heavenly, but I'd love

to work with you too, at some point. We should talk about doing a partnership together." She's so intensely earnest that it throws me. She doesn't seem like the same woman who made comments about my USB T-shirt yesterday.

"Thanks, but I don't see my Heavenly partnership ending anytime soon."

"Oh, well, you should be really careful, then." She nods in the direction of Leo.

I scrunch my brow. "What do you mean?"

She gives me a *you're so silly* look. "Well, isn't there kind of something between the two of you?"

I blink. Is it that obvious? Was it evident from the whispers between us that we were saying *I want you*? Honestly, it probably was.

I do something I hate, but that's necessary for survival. I lie. "There's nothing going on. We've known each other for a long time. He was the best man at my wedding."

There. I hope that'll get her off the scent.

"Oh, thank God there's nothing going on." She wipes a hand dramatically across her forehead. "Because you need to be smart in this environment."

"What do you mean?" A kernel of fear takes root in my chest.

"Aren't you an employee of Heavenly? I'm sure they have a policy that says you can't get involved with the executive who hired you."

I blanch. "Well, I'm not technically an employee. I'm a contractor, so it's different."

"True, though you have to think about not only the letter of the law, but the spirit of the law too. Personally,

I find you can't be too careful these days," she says in a sisters-looking-out-for-each-other way.

As she walks away, I want to trip her.

I want to shout at her.

But I don't have any ground to stand on.

She's right.

You can't be too careful. There aren't any hard and fast rules in place, but the fact is there *are* unwritten rules. And while I'm not worried that Leo would screw me over at work, I do worry how this might look to others—like I slept my way to this opportunity.

I cringe inside at that thought.

And now I have a new wrinkle in the should-I-or-shouldn't-I debate.

The concern isn't only whether it's wise for me to get involved with someone I'm working with while I build my business, but how that involvement might appear to others.

What seemed clear moments ago has once again been muddied.

The same could be said about the clue Kingsley hands us.

They say I'm worth millions. Just weigh me and you'll know. You'll find me by shiny shoes and acorns, underneath the universe, where everything is faster or slower, depending on how you look at it. When you find me, capture the moment with me and your team. Then be sure to add to your collection with all of the above.

Noah stares at me slack-jawed. "What the Derek Jeter is this?"

I'm dumbstruck. I've been riddling my way through the words for five minutes, but I'm back at square one and it's empty. I should know it. But I'm struggling. My decoder ring isn't working well, and maybe it's because RaeLynn's words are ringing in my head, the echo of them occupying all the space that I ought to be devoting to this clue.

Ginny yawns. "Sorry, guys. I'm a bit off my game. Had a late night with my daughter."

"Is everything okay with her?" Noah asks.

Ginny smiles. "She's great. But she possesses a common trait among ten-year-olds. She forgot to tell me we had to make cupcakes for a school project until the very last minute. We were up late baking."

Noah stares at her, perplexed. "Why not just go out and buy the cupcakes?"

Ginny recoils. "I'd be shunned."

"For real?"

Ginny nods. "It's completely verboten. You can't bring in store-bought cupcakes when the class is asked to bake."

"Next time, ask me."

She stares at him incredulously, as if he's begun walking on his hands. "Why?"

"Because I'll help you bake. You can call me anytime."

"But . . . you're twenty-five," she sputters, like that's the natural response to learning someone has baking acumen, when it's actually the first thing on her mind with him—the age difference.

And he knows now. A sly smile spreads on his face. "I get you, Ginny."

"What do you get?"

"You think I'm too young for you. I'll have you know I'm a mature twenty-five, and I can bake my ass off."

"And I'm an old thirty-five."

"Doesn't bother me. I don't even think about it. You shouldn't either."

"I shouldn't think about how young you are?"

"Only to think about how much energy my youth gives me in many areas."

"Is that so?"

"That is *so* so."

And I think he might be wearing her down, erasing her worries about age.

Wait. *Old. Young.* This hunt . . . that's what it's about.

"The past," I whisper to Leo.

"What do you mean?"

"That's what this hunt is about. The tomb, right? And all the other items in the museum yesterday. Obviously, they're items from the past. What if the twist to the hunt is learning from the past? Discovering teamwork or something from the past."

Leo's smile lights up. "That might be it. You could be onto something."

He steps away, paces, furrows his brow. He spins around, heads toward us, muttering under his breath. He's like a detective assembling clues, and it's hella hot.

He passes us again, and as he wears a hole in the concrete, I, too, try to work the problem.

"Maybe it's a famous hotel," Noah offers.

"Or a landmark building," Ginny puts in.

"Maybe it's all of them," I say.

"All of them?" Noah asks.

"Something that combines them." Leo snaps his fingers. "I think I know what it might be. The *weigh me* part is the key." He glances around, making sure the other teams aren't nearby, then pulls us in close and whispers.

I gasp, and I want to smack a big one on his lips because he's so damn clever.

Except I can't do that.

Or really, I shouldn't do that.

RaeLynn's last words underline my every thought.

You can't be too careful these days.

That needs to be my mantra, and I vow to follow it as we rush out of the park, Noah debating the fastest way to Midtown.

When Noah finally settles on a flying carpet—or a cab, if no flying carpet is available—Leo stops in his tracks.

He stares at the ground by the arch. A pink backpack with a rainbow sits forlornly on the concrete. The top is unzipped slightly, revealing purple and pink spiral-bound notebooks and a Pusheen the cat pencil holder. "Guys. Did some kid lose her backpack?"

"I don't know." I bend and take a look at the tag. "Property of Isabelle Grayson." It lists an address a few blocks away.

I look around for any grade-schoolers, but the park is mostly empty of school-age kids, since it's nine thirty. Nor do I spot any young kids searching for a pink bag.

"We should return this," Leo says firmly.

"We should," I say, seconding him. "Doesn't matter if it puts us behind."

Noah groans.

There's a time limit on the scavenger hunt. We have two hours to complete the challenge and send in the photo proof. The team that's fastest and most creative wins the points.

"We can't split up. We can't take the pictures unless the whole team is there. We need to make a decision," Leo says. "Backpack mission or hunt mission?"

"Um. Hate to break it to you. But ticktock." Noah taps his wristwatch.

Ginny stares at Noah. "Hello! Some kid doesn't have her bag for school. She might even have her lunch in there."

He scoffs like that's what he meant to say. "Yeah, exactly. Ticktock, as in, let's get our butts in gear and drop this backpack off at Isabelle's place."

Ginny smiles warmly at him. "I thought that's what you meant." Her words come out a little flirty.

Leo checks the address tag. "Her apartment is a few blocks away. Let's see if there's a doorman we can leave it with, at least."

"Wait." My warning comes out before I expected it to. But the conversation with RaeLynn replays in my head. Would she have planted this backpack? Is this scavenger hunt sabotage? Or worse, did George—sweet, put-upon, beleaguered George . . . Would he have done this to slow down the team in the lead? Both of them are salivating for the prize, albeit for different reasons. I'd hate to think the triplet daddy would do this, but I don't know either one of them. There could be more to this than meets the eye. Isn't there always?

"What is it, Lulu?" Leo asks curiously.

"Do you think this is a trick? Like, some sort of sabotage?"

"Dude, that would make this one cutthroat scavenger hunt," Noah says.

"But it's possible. It could totally be some crazy scheme concocted by those manifesters. The Frodo's people," Ginny suggests, loving the conspiracy idea.

Leo cuts in, his voice confident and commanding.

"Guys, it doesn't matter whether it's a trick or real. Our choices are the same. Leave it or return it. Which one are we doing? I know my decision. What is yours?"

Just like that, he assumes the leadership role fully, and I tuck away my doubt.

All at once, the three of us declare, "Return it."

"I'll do it." Noah reaches for the backpack. "Told you I was Usain Bolt."

And bolt he does. His feet are winged. He's Hermes, flying down the block before anyone can stop him. We jog behind, but he's propelled by jet fuel, racing along the block, stopping briefly to cross the street, then speed-demoning it down the next one.

I point at him. "Holy smokes. That dude can fly."

"He sure can," Ginny says, admiration in her tone.

"Ginny, do I detect a note of you're-seeing-Noah-in-a-new-light in your tone?" Leo asks.

She snaps her gaze toward him. "What? New light?"

"Oh, come on. The two of you clearly have some sort of Sam and Diane vibe."

"You're so old, Leo," Ginny says.

"Ha. *Cheers* is on Netflix. I didn't watch it in the '80s. Also, I turn thirty-three today, so I'm not that old."

"Happy birthday, Leo!" Ginny says.

I stop him, slamming an arm against his. "Today? You turn thirty-three today? You were trying to sneak a birthday past me again?"

"Uh, yeah. I'm not turning one, twenty-one, or one hundred one, so it's no big deal."

"It's your birthday. That's a huge deal, and you never ever let us celebrate it before."

"I'm just not one of those birthday people."

"Whatever. That's crazy talk. I'm making you a cake, and I won't take no for an answer."

"No?" he offers.

I wave it off. "Won't accept it. The only question you should be answering right now is chocolate, marble, black forest, pineapple coconut, or strawberry." I tap my toe, deliberately impatient. "What does the birthday boy want?"

His eyes roam up and down my body, lingering on my throat, my breasts, then finally my lips.

That, right there—the dark look in his brown irises. That's the definition of "melting point." I go from solid woman to liquid desire.

"I want . . . pineapple coconut."

Have it. Have me. Have everything, I want to say.

"I'll make it for you." My voice betrays me. It's breathless, husky. I want to make him a cake, and I want him to have it and eat it too.

Ginny rolls her eyes. "Speaking of vibes . . ."

But before I can ask about vibes, Noah is Forrest Gumping toward us again, pointing down the street. "Isabelle called her building! I talked to the doorman. She's at school. It's two blocks away. I'm going to get it to her before second period."

Then he's Road Runner, flying past us, turning down the next block, and blowing away all the cheetahs in the world.

Ginny watches him, stars in her eyes.

* * *

Despite Noah's best impression of cheetah-meets-Olympic-medalist, we arrive at Grand Central Terminal thirty minutes after we wanted to.

But Isabelle has her backpack, and she told Noah through tears and a smile how happy she was to have it.

Inside the still-grand train station, we rush to the famous clock. It's made of gold, and because of its four opal faces, it's said to be worth $10–$20 million. Hence the *weigh me* part of the clue, since gold is valued by weight.

We take a photo beneath it.

Next, we head to the departure boards, where every train is listed as running one minute earlier than it actually leaves. That's deliberate to accommodate stragglers. We snap another shot of the four of us.

After that, we look skyward, where the stars and the constellations are depicted in gold and green on the ceiling. Another picture.

Finally, we hunt for the marble inlays that appear to be squashed pineapples but are actually acorns, a symbol of the Vanderbilts, who financed the terminal. We find them and take the final photo, sending it in right before the two-hour deadline.

All the items we're unearthing are from years ago. The clock. The ceiling. The departures board. Even the symbol of the Vanderbilts. For a moment, it's as if Kingsley is reading my mind. Making me think about the past. Leo and I have so much past between us.

But even so, I've learned the past isn't what matters anymore.

It's the present and what we do with it.

I don't believe RaeLynn is correct, after all. I definitely don't care if anyone thinks I slept my way to this post. I know the truth. I know *my* truth. I'm here at Heavenly because I'm a damn good chocolatier. I won Kingsley over with my talent. I don't need to prove a thing to anyone but our customers. For them, the chocolate is the only proof needed.

As I gaze at the constellations etched into the ceiling, as I stare at the board where the time isn't always right but is designed to be on our side, and as I take one last look at the clock worth millions, I have to ask myself if time is the answer. If time is bigger than *should I or shouldn't I?*

The past is no longer present. And in my present, my heart wants what my heart wants.

And I am no longer wary of it.

The time is *now*.

As Ginny and Noah debate the ethics of eating food left unmarked in a company's break room fridge—Noah says everything is fair game, while Ginny says gross— they duck into a deli to grab sodas. I grab the opportunity to pull Leo aside between a shoeshine and a flower stand. "Come to my chocolate shop later. Before your cake."

His eyes sweep over me, sending a fresh flurry of tingles through my body. "Chocolate and cake? What are you doing to me, woman?"

The way he says that word—*woman*—is commanding, possessive, and also . . . *crystal clear*.

There's no mistaking his intention when he calls me that.

Out of the corner of my eye, I notice a sign near one

of the shoeshine stands in the terminal. *This used to be the Biltmore Room, and it's being renovated in 2019 to return it to its former glory.*

This is kismet.

This is poetry.

"Do you know what the Biltmore Room used to be?" I ask, a little breathless.

He shakes his head. "No, but I bet you do, little Miss New York Historian."

"It was a room under the Biltmore Hotel where train travelers would meet their sweethearts. And kiss them. It was called The Kissing Room."

His eyes sparkle. "Are you trying to tell me something, Lulu?"

"I believe I am."

He steps closer, crowding me, backing me against the wall between the unmanned shoeshine booth and near the flower stand. He parks one palm against the wall. The other hand fiddles with my necklace. Oh yes, I like Commanding Leo very much.

"Would you like to be kissed, Lulu?" His face is inches from mine. His lips are taunting me with nearness.

All the breath rushes from my body and races down the corridor. "Yes."

"How can I deny you?" He's closer now, his jawline brushing my collarbone, his lips whispering near my throat.

A supernova blasts in my body. "Don't. Don't deny me. Kiss me."

"Are you sure?" His lips barely dust my neck, and I

can't take it. I'm aching exquisitely for him. My lips beg him. My hands grab at him. *I* need him.

"So sure."

He rewards me, his mouth sweeping over mine as he kisses me tenderly and possessively, making the rest of Grand Central Terminal slink away. We might as well be in Alaska or Antarctica, someplace where it's only the two of us, kissing, against the world.

That's how he kisses me.

Like there are no more questions.

No more worries.

No more past.

Only a present where mouths and lips and bodies collide.

He presses so hard against me that I can feel the delicious outline of his erection. I can feel it, and I want more of it. I want all of him. My hands slide around, grabbing his ass, and I nearly groan in ecstasy.

He has the best ass.

So firm, so yummy. So absolutely hold-on-able.

"Nice butt," I murmur in between kisses.

"Nice everything," he whispers then devours me more, and I'm quite sure I'll be sporting some serious whisker burn and equally sure I don't care.

Because this is why kissing was invented.

For moments like this.

I can't get enough of him. My body has a mind of its own, and I start to move and grind against him. To rub against that ridge, to squeeze those cheeks.

My self-control gallops away, and I'm ready to beg him to take me here, to take me anywhere.

But a throat clears.

When my eyes snap open to see the shoeshine man setting polish on a leather chair, my face flushes red.

"Goddamn Kissing Room," he mutters, and that's our cue to get the hell out of there.

Or we're going to have to rename The Kissing Room —The Home Run Room.

26

LULU

When we return to the starting point of the hunt, I don't mind that our team fell far behind today.

Because we felt more like a team than we did yesterday, and because tonight I'm seeing Leo.

No matter what RaeLynn says, getting involved with Leo isn't a bad idea. It's never been about the work. It's never been about Heavenly. It's been about me, rebuilding my life, refurbishing my business.

After the teams fan out, returning to their corporate homes, I grab him and pull him aside. "It's not foolish anymore."

He quirks up his lips. "Is that so? Did you remove the seal of foolishness sometime today?"

I nod, smiling widely. "I did. It's gone."

"What changed?"

"Nothing and also everything."

He laughs. "That's broad and vague at the same time."

I shrug. "I know, but the truth is, it's simple. I

thought about it. I weighed it. I decided it's more foolish not to see what might come of you and me."

"Pun intended?"

"Oh, I hope the coming won't be a pun."

"I promise there will be nothing punny in that department. But seriously, last night you were reticent."

"I know. But life is short, Leo. I've been worried that in order to build my career, I needed to focus *only* on my career, but if I do that, I'll miss out on another part of life—on us. Just like I missed out on my career beforehand. I don't want to keep missing out, on either side. And even if RaeLynn tries to whisper insidious things in my ear, the reality is you aren't my boss, and I'm not your employee, and this—us, whatever this is— will only get in the way of our business deal if we let it get in the way."

He arches a brow. "RaeLynn?"

I tell him briefly what she said to me earlier. "And then she was so curious how we knew each other. I bet she goes on Facebook and stalks me tonight. But guess what? I have nothing to hide. In fact, I think we should tell Kingsley that I want to bang you."

He cracks up. "That's what you think we should tell her? I mean, it's supremely awesome, but I think maybe it's not the best approach."

I tap-dance my fingers over his chest. "Fine. But I will be thinking about banging you when we tell her, let me assure you."

He grabs my hand, squeezes, and says in a smoky, sexy voice, "That makes me very reassured."

* * *

Quickly, we find Kingsley, who's chatting with her sister in the park, debating whether *Grey's Anatomy* jumped the shark in season five, six, or seven.

I jump in. "Season eleven. It was that episode when—"

Kingsley holds up a bejeweled hand. "Don't say it. I like to pretend that never happened."

I mime zipping my lips. Then I unzip them. "Actually, do you have a minute for something else? Something much more uplifting than a show that rips out your heart, then eviscerates it, then boils it with lobsters?"

"Of course. What can I do for you?" She steps away from her sister, and the three of us grab seats at an empty chess table.

I inhale deeply, ready to tell her, when Leo speaks.

"Lulu and I want to date. Is that going to be a problem?"

I burst into sunshine, loving that he jumped first.

Kingsley's lips twitch, and she looks from him to me, me to him, like a seesaw. She chuckles. A little harder. Then louder, until she covers her mouth.

Kingsley waves her hand as if she's trying to rein in her laughing. Eventually, she collects herself. "I'm sorry, but that was cuter than otters holding hands. You two are going on a poster in the subway for *How to Date without Tinder, Cinder, and Hinder.*"

"For the record, Hinder is the best. It just flat-out stops you from all dates," Leo says, deadpan.

I dive in, going along with it. "Admittedly, Cinder was kind of fun, but eventually they all went up in flames."

Kingsley's eyes play tennis spectator between the two of us. "That's what I'm talking about. This thing."

"Actually, we're heading to the transit authority next to have our photo taken," Leo adds, keeping up the routine.

That's the best part—we can tell her and do it like us, like two old friends, finishing each other's sentences and making jokes.

Kingsley hoots then slaps a hand on the table. "Listen, I knew there was something cooking between the two of you. I knew it all along. And I am so delighted that I'd like to take credit. So, is that cool? Credit given to *moi*?"

"Take it. You can have all the credit you want."

"Excellent. Now, I will only say two things." Her expression turns serious, her tone pure boardroom. "If this explodes and turns into all sorts of relationship carnage and Facebook relationship statuses revoked, and if that affects the partnership, I will be a new shade of livid you won't want to see."

Leo parts his lips, but Kingsley is not a woman to be interrupted.

"That means I expect you to behave like adults, whether this works out or not. And Leo, you need to remember that Lulu is a very important business partner. Treat her with respect and kindness. And don't be a dick."

"I'm not a dick."

"I know, but I have to say it."

She looks to me. "And Lulu, this man is inscrutable. How you broke down his walls is beyond me, but kudos to you, and I expect the same as well.

Behave like adults whether this goes badly or swimmingly."

I squeeze Leo's hand. "I vote for swimmingly."

"Me too," Leo says, and as Kingsley chats about her expectations for the line, I let myself enjoy how easy this was—telling her.

Then again, telling her was never supposed to be hard.

There was never a line in the corporate sand forbidding the two of us.

The line was personal, drawn by me, and I've undrawn it and I'm ready to step over it.

Kingsley folds her hands. "Now that we have that out of the way, I want you to know I fully expect a wedding invite. I'd also like to sing at the wedding, and I hope you'll name your firstborn after me."

Leo's jaw drops.

She flaps her hands, gesturing from me to him. "Don't worry. If you have a son, you can name him Kingston. For the record, you'd make beautiful babies. I sure hope you're getting to that soon. I'd like babies in the office. I'd like to throw a baby shower. I'd like to have a day care at work. My own children haven't given me grandkids yet, and that kind of neglect needs to stop soon."

I laugh, and Leo laughs lightly too, and it's not one of those high-pitched nervous man laughs, but an easy one, like he doesn't think any of these ideas are crazy. He taps his temple as if he's filing away the info. "Duly noted."

I make a note of it as well.

Because I want that too.

Well, not yet.

But someday.

Maybe even someday soon.

And tonight I want that thing you do that makes them.

27

LEO

I meet up with Dean at the gym during lunch. As we climb endless steps, I give him the bare minimum update, and he raises a most curious brow.

"And does this mean you'll be telling her the truth, the whole truth, and nothing but the truth? As in, *Lulu, I had it bad for you for years, and by 'years,' I mean for-fucking-ever.*"

"That'd be a hard no."

"That little detail will remain vault-level intel?"

I tap my skull. "One hundred percent."

"And why's that?"

I feign baring my soul to her. "Oh hello, Lulu. I think you're the cat's pajamas, and I have for years. Including, but not limited to, the day I met you, every time we hung out, and oh, also during your wedding to my best bud. Want to bang tonight?"

Dean pretends to swoon. "You had me at 'hello.'"

I stare at him as I climb another level on the

machine. "You do know I wasn't whacking off to her under the table at the wedding reception?"

"But after the reception when you were home alone, right?"

I shoot eels from my eyes at him.

"Fine, fine. I'm not saying you ought to serve it all up tonight and wrap it with a pretty bow. But is it right going into a relationship, or whatever this is, without being completely honest?"

"There's honesty, and then there's stupidity."

"Why is it stupid to let on that you fancied her for the better part of a decade? It's kind of romantic." He bats his lashes. "*It's you. It's always been you.* They just don't make shows like *Friends* anymore. Was there anything better than Rachel and Ross finally getting together?"

I point furiously at him, as if his words have turned into alphabet soup in the air. "That. Right there. Life isn't a *Friends* episode. And what if Ross was creepy? What if maybe in retrospect it made him look like a pathetic sad sack?"

"Ross? Never."

"I'm serious. Imagine me telling her. I'm the guy, then, who harbored a massive fucking secret from his best friend—and also from her, and she's a good friend too. A great friend."

"You make a fair point. I suppose the alternative is you could suffocate under the weight of the secret forever and ever. Do that."

I sigh heavily as I climb the five hundredth set of stairs. "I don't want her to look back on everything we've done together and scrutinize it through the lens of this new information. And I don't want to freak her out and make her wonder if every little thing I've said to her meant something else." My blood heats, boiling like a kettle left on too long, and I'm whistling. "I just want to move on from the past. I can't keep dredging it up."

He hits the button to slow the cycle on his Stair-Master. "Yeah, I get that. Embrace the present. But soon enough, it'll come out. Just think about it."

I relent. "I will."

"But one more question. Why are you going for it now? If last night was a line in the sand, what changed today? Or did you get too horny to handle?"

I make a jerking gesture with my hand. "I can handle horny, thank you very much."

"Bloody hell if I can." He looks at his watch. "Speaking of, Fitzgerald has a game tonight. I need to go give him his good luck charm."

"Do I even want to know what that is?"

"Oh, you might. It's when—"

I wave him off. "Goodbye, Dean."

"Mark my words. You'll be wondering what it is."

* * *

His question weighs on me the rest of the workday. Not what good luck charm Dean gives to his husband, but the other one.

Why am I going for it now?

As I replay the scavenger hunt earlier today, my answer to *why now?* lies in something unexpected. I want her to know, so I send a text in the afternoon, choosing directness.

Leo: Do you want to know what changed for me?

Lulu: Of course.

Leo: Noah.

Lulu: What does Noah have to do with anything?

Leo: When he grabbed the backpack and took off running. He just went for it.

Lulu: Am I the backpack?

Leo: I think you might be the backpack, Lulu.

Lulu: Are you going to go for me?

Leo: Yes.

I set my phone to silent and power through the rest of the workday. When I turn it back on, I find a missed call from Tripp's mom.

My finger hovers over her contact info, and I'm *this* close to returning her call. But it can wait till tomorrow. I don't want to be in that world tonight.

When I return to my place to shower, I walk past a picture of Tripp and me at his restaurant, some random night, and make a choice—to put him out of my mind.

Tonight, I choose not to think about that promise I made.

28

LULU

The scent of truffles enrobes me. Sensual and rich, the aroma floods my nostrils as I craft a new batch to take to Kingsley tomorrow. Flavors of caramel, vanilla, and pistachios float through the air. Corinne Bailey Rae plays on my phone, drifting through the closed shop.

The door creaks open, and I nearly shriek when I see a familiar face—warm crinkles against dark blue eyes, dark-blond hair curling at the ends, and a grin just for me. I drop my tools on the counter and rush over to throw my arms around my best friend. Emotion slams into me all at once.

"You're here!"

"Whoa! Did you forget I was coming back to town?"

"I just missed you."

"My flight arrived early from Chicago," he says, mentioning the site of his most recent hotel meeting. "Figured I should at least stop by and see my business partner before I go out on a hot date tonight."

I let go of him to check out his shoes. Black loafers. "And you're not wearing Crocs tonight."

"Did I say I was wearing my loafers on my date? I have a brand-new pair of Birkenstocks I'll be slipping into. Did I tell you I'm switching to Birkenstocks for the ladies?"

I cover his mouth. "You didn't say that. We will never speak of your footwear again."

"Flip-flops?" He tries to speak around my hand, and I shake my head.

"How about those foot gloves with the rubber-covered toes?"

I slump dramatically to the floor like the Wicked Witch melting, fitting since I'm wearing a green dress. "I can't go on."

Laughing, he offers me a hand, tugs me up, then whispers, "Confession: I'm wearing the loafers tonight. All because of you."

"Praise the Lord!" I thrust my arms into the air. "Also, it's so good to see you again. Business is going great here. The shop manager is awesome, and I've been trying to spend as much time as I can here, all while handling Heavenly stuff. But let's talk about how awesome you are. Sounds like you were a rock star in Miami, and in Vegas, and in Chicago?"

"I sealed the deal with the hotel in Florida. Paperwork is all done. They want to carry Lulu's Chocolates in their swank, chichi lobby shop. Flamingo-shaped chocolate for the win. And things are looking good with the Vegas hotel too, and the Chicago one."

I grab his cheeks and kiss his forehead. "I love you, I love you, I love you."

"And I love you. But I'm only here for a few minutes."

"Who's your hot date with? When I saw you in Miami last week, you mentioned a mystery woman. Is there a mystery woman in New York too?"

"Please. I am a one-woman man."

"And a one mystery-woman man?"

"Indeed."

"So who *is* the mystery woman?"

He arches a brow playfully. "Don't you want to know."

"I do. That's why I asked!"

He squares his shoulders and takes a deep, exaggerated breath. "My grandma."

"Aren't you the perfect grandson?"

"Let's just say I've been inspired to take her out. We have a date with Puccini."

"And the perfectly cultured grandson."

"That is true. Now, before I don my tux, hit me up with some sugar. Give me some of those new flavors so I know what I'm wheeling and dealing."

I show him the chocolates, and he tries a few, rolling his eyes in pleasure. "You always do that. How will I ever know if these are truly good?"

"I guess you'll just have to trust me. Would I lie to you?"

Cameron wouldn't lie to me. Cameron has always been fully honest. That's why I spit out the news that's bubbling up inside me, because I'm dying to know what he thinks. "I think I'm falling for Leo."

"Let me just slam on the brakes right now." He

makes a screeching sound, then shakes his head like a horse, trying to clear his thoughts.

He stares at me with bulging eyes, his voice hitting a few octaves higher than his deep, delicious baritone. "What did you just say?"

"I'm falling for Leo." Saying it does crazy things to my heart. Makes the organ tap-dance around in my chest. "I think he feels the same. We're going to date. We even told Kingsley at Heavenly. It's nuts, isn't it?"

"Nuts is when you wear muumuus and slippers to work. This is downright bananas, blowing-my-mind. You are aware he was the best man at your wedding?"

I shoot him a curious stare. I'm surprised he isn't happier. "Gee, thanks. I'd nearly forgotten he was my ex's best friend for ten years and counting. Want to tattoo on me that you don't think I should get involved with him?"

He stares at me down the bridge of his nose. "That's not what I said, and you know it."

"Then what are you saying?"

"I'm saying this is big. Ocean-size big. This is the-sea-turned-purple-and-is-floating-with-sapphires big."

"Take me to your ocean, please."

He squeezes my arm. "Are you really falling for him?"

My heart trampolines in my chest. "Yes. Falling like night falls, like waterfalls, like rainfalls." But something gnaws at me, pokes its concerns into my shoulder. "But what about the three-legged stool analogy? Were we better as a three-legged stool?"

"Maybe the three of you were good as the Three Musketeers. But I think sometimes you told yourself that you were a threesome. At the end of the day, you went home with only one person. When it comes to love, most of the time a pair of aces beats three of a kind."

That's what I want to be with Leo—a pair. "So the analogy no longer applies."

"It no longer applies for many reasons. Most of all, now there are two, and two is something of a perfect number. What do you want the two of you to be?"

That's what I want to explore. "We're still figuring it out, but something more than friends, for sure. A part of me thinks I should feel guilty, but I don't. I don't feel an ounce of guilt."

He holds up a hand to high-five. "Guilt is a terrible emotion. Guilt strangles you. Guilt wraps its horrible tentacles around you and squeezes away your joy. That's a scientifically proven fact."

"Like, it's been tested and verified?"

"Absolutely. Studies show that being stymied by guilt makes music sound tinny, spicy food taste bland, and champagne go flat. You don't want that, do you?"

I shudder.

"Guilt also makes it impossible to move forward. And you're not someone who can't move forward. Are you?"

I shake my head, but even so, a slab of worry slams into my stomach. "But I'm scared."

"What are you scared of? Being with Leo? Because it sure sounds like he might feel the same way you do."

"I'm scared I'm still the same girl I was before."

"What girl was that?"

I let all the fears spill from my mouth in a wild

heap. "The poet, the dreamer, the one who listens to her heart, not her head. I've always been that girl. What if I haven't changed? What if I haven't learned? What if I'm still her?"

Cameron runs a hand over my arm, comforting me. "Look at you in your emerald-green dress making truffles for a company called Heavenly. Telling your best friend not to wear Birkenstocks to the opera tonight. Listening to Corinne Bailey Rae as you make something decadently sweet. You're a big red beating heart on the sleeve. You're probably always going to be that woman. But is she such a bad person to be?"

The image he paints is lovely, and I want to crawl into it, curl up, and live inside it. Still, worry is a super-hero tonight, with super strength. "But shouldn't I be someone who makes decisions with her head?"

"Some people make decisions with their head, some with their gut, and some with their heart. If I look back on the last ten years of your life, I'd still see a fierce warrior. I'd see an iron strength. And I'd say, too, that your heart's been in the right place." He taps my sternum. "Maybe it's not such a bad idea to lead with your heart."

Mine thumps loudly, bursting with gratitude for my friend. "Have I mentioned I love you?"

He winks. "A few times. Also, I love you just the way you are. And I think love is always worth a chance, even when you've already been through the fire." He tilts his head, studying me. "But promise me one thing."

"What's that?"

He levels me with his gaze, a shade of intensity I've never seen before blazing across his eyes. "Don't ever settle for second best. You wound up playing that part with your ex, and it's a part you never knew you were going to have to take on. Hell, you weren't even the understudy, but it's the role you were unexpectedly cast in when his mistress became his true love."

My throat squeezes, tightening with tears. "I know."

"You stood by him. You helped him. But you were never his first. This time around? You deserve to be someone's first and someone's only. Got that, Lu?"

I swallow the tears whole, lifting my chin, letting his strength fuel me. "I believe that."

After Cameron says good night, I finish the batch of truffles, singing along to the music, imagining the night unfolding, letting the riot in my heart lead me on.

A little later, my phone pings with a note from Leo, telling me he's outside.

I'm buzzed with anticipation, floating on a cloud of possibility as I wipe my chocolate-covered hands on my red polka-dot apron and answer the door.

29

LEO

If I looked back and listed the moments of the last twenty-four hours on a spreadsheet, detailing the specific points that led me here, like running a hand through wet, freshly-showered hair, adjusting my collar in the mirror, and putting on aftershave, I suppose I would have to start with choices.

The choice to tell her I couldn't stop thinking about her.

The choice to say yes when she invited me over.

The choice to text with her earlier.

But, truth be told, I suppose I've always known, if given the chance, I would do this. I would walk right into whatever opportunity she gave me.

I leave my apartment, reach the shop, and text her that I'm here, wild anticipation curling through me.

Seconds later, she comes into view, all green and curly blonde and bright, a splash of color and exuberance.

She wears a smile like it's a tattoo, and her smile jumps through the glass and lands in my hands.

She opens the door, lets me in, then locks it. Grabbing my hand, she tugs me behind the counter to the back of the shop, out of sight of the windows. She sits me down in a chair, spins around like a whirling dervish, then hands me a tray with chocolates.

"Try this." A truffle meets my lips, and I take a bite. It melts on my tongue. Pineapple, coconut, and chocolate spread into my mouth, chased by a dash of I-have-a-secret-to-share-with-you. I groan in pleasure. "It's delicious."

"I made it for you, birthday boy."

"So I get birthday chocolate from the chocolatier?"

"Of course. You deserve all the sweets. But there are more at my place."

My place.

The invitation hovers in the air, flashing like a billboard.

"I bet this chocolate tastes good on your hands too." I reach for her finger, and I lick the rest of the chocolate off. Her eyes seem to float closed, and when she opens them, she sways toward me. "Leo, you can't do that in here."

"Why not?" I reach for another finger and lick the chocolate from that too, slowly, enjoying every inch of Lulu and sweetness.

"Because it's going to drive me too crazy."

"Is that what you want? To be driven crazy?"

I draw one more finger to my mouth.

She moans. "I think you know what I want."

"I do know."

My entire body is buzzed from this heady knowledge. It's like I'm both living and watching this moment. The me that's watching is staring in disbelief. The me that's living it is thinking how it's so much better than all those years of fantasies.

And I want to live in the moment. The absolutely real and surreal moment of licking chocolate off Lulu. I stand, gesturing to her hair. "Take your hair down."

She unclips her locks. They fall in wild corkscrew curls around her face.

"Take off your apron."

She does as asked, setting it down on the counter behind her. "Do you want me to take off my dress?"

I gaze heavenward. "Happy birthday to me."

She laughs. "So that's a yes?"

"It's a yes, but not yet."

"Tell me what you want for your birthday. Tell me what I can give you."

My heart drums against my chest. It's too big for my body. It occupies too much space. At last, I say words that I've held tight inside me for years. Words that I shoved down and vanquished.

I cup her cheeks. "Give me you."

She trembles. "You can have me."

I savor the way those words sound. How they imprint on the air. At last, the hurricane of Lulu has made landfall, and I want to be in its eye.

But even though I want her more than the world right now, last night weighs on me. I don't want her to enter this—whatever it is—reluctantly.

"You're sure you're not worried anymore about us

working together, about your focus, about anything at all?"

She presses her hands to my chest, and I sizzle from her touch. The more she touches me, the less I'll be able to think logically. "I'm more worried about you walking out the door when I tell you I want to climb you like a tree."

Laughing, I clasp her hands and squeeze. "There will be no walking out."

She squeezes back, sealing a new promise—one between the two of us. "So can you handle it? That I want you? After all we've been through together? You can handle the fact that, somehow, we're here now and all of sudden we have these crazy feelings for each other that can't be denied?"

I wince privately at those words—there is nothing sudden about my feelings for her. But she doesn't need to know that. Come to think of it, I don't think she wants to know that. I run the backs of my fingers over her jawline. "I'm pretty sure I can handle both the tree climbing and the way we want each other."

I reach for her hair, threading a hand through it, amazed at the softness of her curls, astonished that after all these years, I'm touching her the way I've longed to. I dip my head to her neck, inhaling her coconut scent, her sugar skin, her sweetness. I pull back to look her in her gloriously mismatched eyes. "But can you handle that I want you? That I feel this way for you? That I can't stop thinking of you?"

There. I don't have to unpack a trunkful of old feelings. I can share the new ones and be just as truthful, if not more.

She laughs. "Not only can I handle it, I want it."

I try to capture a mental snapshot of this moment, to record it for my own personal time capsule, because it's shocking when all your darkest, dirtiest, most powerful dreams come true. It's too much and it's not enough at the same time.

I hold her face. "I've been thinking all day about kissing you."

"Kiss me all night."

With that, I crush my lips to hers.

Our kiss yesterday was an exploration. It was a curiosity, a test. This kiss is a declaration. It's a written record of what's in my heart. I'm kissing the woman I've been in love with for years, and who I'm falling in love with all over again.

Only it feels like it's the first time, because this time around, she's mine.

I kiss her hard, pouring all of those feelings into the way my lips consume hers. She kisses me back as if she's falling in love with me too, and it is the most wondrous thing I've ever experienced in my life.

I lift her up, wrap her legs around my hips, and bring her to the wall, pressing my body against her.

I don't think I'll ever get enough of her lips. I don't think I'll ever get enough of her. I'm making up for so much lost time.

Her tongue sweeps into my mouth, and her hands grab at my back and my shirt, untucking it from my jeans. "I want to touch you."

I'm lit up. "That can be arranged."

I set her down, and she runs her hands over my shirt, making quick work of the buttons, spreading open the fabric. She presses her hands against my chest.

I hiss from pleasure as my brain crackles like an old radio tuning in signals from space. I groan from the stark and wonderful reality of Lulu touching me.

I unzip the back of her dress, letting the little straps fall down her shoulders, exposing her pale skin and the freckles on her shoulder. Those coppery freckles—I've studied them surreptitiously. Every time she wore a strapless dress to a club, a bikini on the beach, or a top that sloped down.

So often I've wanted to map them with my lips. Now I have the chance, so I do, savoring every moment of my lips on her skin, tracing her collarbone, traveling to the hollow of her throat, then blazing a path of kisses up her neck.

Lulu moans and groans, stretching like a cat as I kiss her skin. This is new data that I file away. It belongs to me, how Lulu responds as I kiss her. How she sways and murmurs. How she trembles and shudders.

Every move she makes unlocks me more. Makes me want to say something. To say everything.

I'm in love with you, I want to tell her.

I'm in love with you so much it's absurd, but let's be absurd together and kiss and fuck and love each other like it's finally our time.

I'm in love with you again, the second time around, and it's like a tsunami. It's pulling me under. Pulling me closer to you.

I cup her jaw, bring her lips to mine, and kiss her because kissing her makes me shut up. It helps me swallow down those dangerous words. There's no way I can tell her I was in love with her before.

Focus.

Focus on the here and now.

I do that, kissing her as our hands feverishly explore each other. I tug down the top of her dress, exposing her bra then unhooking it, letting it fall to the floor of her chocolate shop.

Breasts.

Glorious, fantastic breasts.

Breasts that I can touch and squeeze and knead.

I take them in my hands, savoring the view of Lulu stretching her neck as she seems to revel in the sensation.

"Take my dress off now, Leo."

Somebody bring me some water. I'm going to burn this chocolate shop down with the fire roaring in my body.

I slide her dress down farther, until it's an emerald linen heap. She's wearing zebra panties, and they are the cutest, unsexiest panties I've ever seen. Laughter bursts from my throat as I stare at the striped horse on her crotch.

"Is that a zebra or are you just happy to see me?"

"Why don't you find out how happy I am?"

I run my hand over the fabric. "Zebra panties are officially the best thing ever."

"Wait till you see my dolphin undies."

"I'd like to get to know the whole safari and maritime collection."

She laughs, and here we are laughing as we touch each other's bodies for the first time.

I stop laughing as I cup her between her legs,

feeling the dampness that's soaked through the cotton panel where my fingers slide. I close my eyes for a moment because this is too much.

My bones hum. My mind buzzes.

Lulu wants this. Lulu wants *me*.

As I glide my fingers across her, she moans, and I realize she's not far off. That knowledge thrills me.

I whisper in her ear, "Can I taste you?"

She opens her eyes. "I was hoping you would."

"Is that so?"

Her eyes are wild beacons of desire, shining with the neon words *please, please, please.* "Yes. Will you?"

"You don't have to ask. The answer for you is always yes."

I kneel on the tiles, pull down her panties, and help her step out of them. Raising my face, I look up, drinking in the sight of her naked body, her soft flesh, her trembling skin, and her desire.

She glistens.

For me.

Only for me.

As I kiss her inner thigh, she trembles.

It hits me fantastically. That, right there. That tremble. That's for me too.

I switch to her other thigh, and she rewards me with a shudder. I watch her, her breasts heaving, her hands rising up to her hair. She threads them through her locks, and it's so fucking sensual it nearly breaks my resolve to make her come first, and many times.

But my resolve is steel, and Lulu is melting under my mouth.

I flick my tongue up her thigh, closer and closer.

The sounds she makes should be illegal. Moans and groans of desire, so lustful, so heady, fall on my ears, and it's no lie to say I've never been this turned on.

Then I kiss her where she wants me most, and it's everything.

It's all the things.

It's a storm, it's the sky, it's the moon.

She cries out. "Oh my God, that's soooo good."

That cry of pleasure? That belongs to my ears.

That full-body shudder? It belongs to me.

Her hands drop to my hair, curl around my head, and yank me close. "More, more," she pants.

Mine, mine, I think.

As I flick my tongue across her wetness, all these sensations, all her reactions, go into a new memory bank in my head. I can drive Lulu crazy. I can make her feel this way.

Every noise, every murmur, everything she's doing right now is because of me, for me, and is mine alone.

Maybe that makes me horribly selfish. But maybe that's what I need to accept that this is finally happening.

And it does happen.

It doesn't take Lulu long at all. I kiss her and lick her and devour her like she's better than chocolate, better than pineapple, better than coconut. Because she is. Because she's fucking Lulu Diamond, and she's the best thing I've ever tasted and the person I've wanted most in my entire life. And she's right here, wanting me as much as I want her.

As I kiss her, she pulls me closer until she's coming on my tongue, saying my name over and over. I'm in another world. Another realm. She tastes like heaven, and she sounds like every filthy dream I've ever had about her.

She sounds like sex and love and desire and every wish I've ever had.

I hold her hips, keeping her steady as I rise, recording the look of rapture on her face, how her lips are parted, how her breath is still coming fast.

"I need to be inside you, Lulu. I need it so badly."

She opens her eyes. "Come home with me."

* * *

I'm not sure how we make it to her place, but we do, and ten minutes later, we're inside her apartment, and I'm undressing her again, and she's taking my clothes off for the first time, and everything is a flurry, a feverish race to the finish line.

Somewhere along the way, she tells me she's clean and on the pill and I tell her I'm all clear too, and when she's naked in her living room, every animal instinct takes over. I hoist her up, toss her over my shoulder, and carry her to the bedroom.

I turn on the light, but I see only her. I don't give a flying fuck what her room looks like.

She's all I want to see.

I'm going to watch her face as I fuck her.

I want to see what every moan and tremble of pleasure looks like.

She climbs up on the bed, and she's shuddering.

"Spread your legs."

She does, and a landmine of pleasure explodes in

my body. Every nerve ending is raw, crying out. She's so sensual and so ready.

I crawl over her, straddling her, poised for entry.

She grabs my erection.

It's like a jolt of electricity. Her touch shoots through my body. I'm so turned on I could light the city —I could power the entire grid. Lulu's hand is rubbing my shaft, and it's not fucking fair that it should feel this good, and it's also the most fair thing in the universe.

Because it's absolutely incredible.

Her hand is soft and strong, and it's like she holds my heart in it. With every stroke up my cock, I lose a little more willpower and she turns the key in the lock a little farther.

The words start to rattle free from their cage.

It's you.

It's been you forever.

That won't do.

I bat her hand away, taking both of hers in mine then pinning them above her head.

She stares up at me with wide, eager eyes, then whispers, "Make love to me."

And like that, she's reaching into the dark, secret place inside me. "That's all it'll ever be."

Then I sink inside her, and the pleasure—the sheer, unadulterated pleasure—of being home blots out the world.

There is no room for any other thought.

No space for anything else.

But this.

I thrust deep into her, and she cries out.

I swivel my hips, and she shouts my name.

I grind and thrust and pump, and she pants, moans, groans.

We're in sync, fucking and loving, loving and fucking.

She's taking me to the ends of the earth, to the edge of pleasure, and I'm doing the same to her.

But it's not enough.

I need to get closer.

"Lulu," I breathe.

"Yeah?"

"Bring your knees up."

She pulls them up higher, opening wider. "Like this?"

"Just like that."

I adjust us so her legs drape over my shoulders, and this is fitting, this is how we're meant to be together.

"I love this," she murmurs, and the verb seeps into me.

Love.

With her under me, bent up and beautiful, I can control everything, including the revelation of the vintage of my emotions.

Because fucking her is everything.

It's everything I imagined it to be.

And soon, we're rushing, racing, chasing each other to the cliff.

She falls first, chanting my name, calling out God's name, announcing her pleasure. Then it's my turn, and I'm less coherent. I'm all grunts and sizzles as the wires crackle and pleasure burns, detonating in every cell in my body.

It's enough to loosen the iron grip on my words.

A minute later, I'm holding her, stroking her hair as she murmurs sweet nothings.

That was incredible.

That was amazing.

That was so good.

And I whisper something that is wholly and wonderfully true. "I'm so in love with you."

30

LULU

I wear my heart on my sleeve.

I am the girl who believes in big, messy, beautiful love.

The kind that glows, spills over, and shines like a treasure chest rich with rubies, rife with sapphires.

I'm not scared.

I'm not afraid of feeling love again.

Because this—the way I want to curl myself around this strong, sensitive man, the way I want to smother him in kisses and sling quips in his direction and make him spicy peppers and run my hand over his sandpaper stubble and discover all the things going on inside his head—is *new*.

I don't want to compare men. I don't want to balance and weigh loves.

Leo is everything I thought he would be.

Because I know him.

There's no darkness to be revealed in the bright

light of morning. There's no madness that'll seep through the cracks.

Leo is who he says he is. The ingredients that comprise him are the ones I want most in the recipe for a man to love—he's loyal, he's kind, he's funny, he's caring. And he's sober.

Also, he's one hell of a fiend in the sack.

I climb over him, cup his cheeks, and look into his soulful brown eyes. "I'm so in love with you."

He smiles at me from the inside of his soul. "Yeah?"

I drop a kiss to his nose. "Yes. So much yes. It's crazy and wonderful, and I'm kind of ridiculously in love with you. How the hell did this happen?" I burst into laughter. "Someone tell me how this happened. It's fantastic!"

He laughs, threads a hand in my hair, and tugs me close for a kiss. "It was time."

I furrow my brow, my laughter ceasing like a faucet has turned it off. "What do you mean, 'It was time'?" Something sounds portentous in his words, and I flash back to my mother's comment—*years in his eyes*.

Has he always?

He swallows, perhaps taken aback, then clears his throat. "I mean, we've known each other. You know?"

"Right. But not always like . . ." I don't know how to finish the thought or why it stuns me so much. But maybe it's because I love the newness of this. I love the us-ness of this. I love that we can be a two-legged stool. Not a three-legged one with one leg sliced off.

I want him and me, and me and him, and no one else. I want this new love to belong to us.

"I just meant, the time was right because we've been friends."

"Oh. Right. Yes." That feels true and good. That makes sense to me. That's *years*. "It's the same for me. I've been friends with you for so long. And now here you are in my life in a new way, and boom. Everything inside me blooms for you. Like a sunflower coming to life. You've turned me into a sunflower."

He chuckles once more, and I love that. I want to catch his laughter and put it in a jar, then sneak a whiff of it every time I need a pick-me-up.

"Kiss me, sunflower. And don't stop."

I kiss him madly. Ravenously. I kiss him so much it leads to more and more. It leads to him whispering roughly to me, telling me to sit on his face, to ride him, to fuck him hard.

I'm only too glad to oblige.

And he seems happy to oblige me in other ways too, sliding me under him once more and driving me out of my mind with pleasure.

When we're drunk on sex and spent, I pat his belly. "You've earned your cake."

"You really made one?"

I shoot him a *did you doubt me* look. "I take birthday cake very seriously."

"When did you make this?"

I shrug happily. "I had time after the hunt, so I baked it here, worked on recipes while it cooled, then headed to the shop."

"You're a machine."

"Where there's a will, there's a way." I trot out to the kitchen, slice two pieces of the cake I slipped away to bake this afternoon, then bring the plates back to bed. I hand him a fork and his slice.

He dives in and chews. "Best birthday cake ever." He glances behind him at the clock. "Best birthday ever."

I look him over from head to toe. "I'd say. And here you are celebrating it in your birthday suit. You've always looked good in suits."

"That so?"

"I remember noticing how good you looked in your Tom Ford suit at the chocolate show."

He arches a brow. "You noticed my suit at the show?"

"I noticed how handsome you looked in it."

His smile is an entirely new variety. He lowers his head, grinning like he's incandescently pleased with this intel.

I decide to make him even happier, because I think I can. I gesture to his naked flesh. "But this one you're wearing tonight? It's definitely my favorite suit you own."

His grin shifts to decadent mode now. "I'm happy to wear it for you anytime."

"And I'll be taking you up on that." I take another bite then shift gears. "Why have you never been big on your birthday? I want to know you. I want to know all the things I don't know."

"I never had much growing up. There were years when we had very little."

"You didn't celebrate your birthday at all?"

"We did. My mom always made sure we had something, whether it was a small gift like a Matchbox car, or something a little bigger, like a book. But because it was hard for my parents, I didn't want anyone to ever feel like they had to do something for me. That's why my birthday was never a big deal to me."

"I like doing things for you."

"I like doing things for you and to you." He finishes his slice and sets the plate on my nightstand. Then his stomach growls.

"Cake not enough for you?"

"I guess I'm still hungry."

"I'm terrible, since I didn't feed you dinner. Do you want to order something? Pizza, Thai, Vietnamese . . . there's a fun place down the street that has sliders."

"Sliders. When did sliders become a thing?"

I laugh as I take another bite of my cake. "I think it was because of White Castle. That *Harold and Kumar Go to White Castle* movie?"

"Ah, yes. They started calling them sliders. Why not call them mini burgers though?"

"Because mini burgers doesn't sound as sexy as sliders?"

Leo's face straightens. "Lulu, I need to tell you something."

"What's that?"

"Sliders are not sexy."

I put down my plate. "What's sexy to you?"

He reaches for me, flips me to my stomach, and kisses my spine. "You. Literally everything about you."

"Everything? You sure about that?"

"I'm positive, and just because you doubted me, I'll prove it to you."

He proceeds to travel up and down my body, naming all the sexy spots.

Back of your knee.
Inside of your arm.
Right there above your belly button.
The shell of your ear.
Your ankle, dear God, your ankle.
The dimple at the top of your ass.

I shiver as he continues his soliloquy, lavishing attention on my hungry, greedy body.

Somehow, he wrings another orgasm out of me, and then I give him one too, and it feels like the world is a string of pearls at our feet.

Like everything is possible if we're in this together.

* * *

That floaty, bubbly sensation carries me into the next day, to Strawberry Fields in Central Park, where we meet the team, grab our clue, and, like super decoder spies, run through options.

Add me up and I'm like a two by two, climb me and you'll be lucky twice . . . Look inside and you'll see a famous flyer, look out and you'll see nearly everything. I'm arguably the prettiest, and I'm inarguably a masterpiece of a movement.

"Is it a Monet?" Noah asks. "Wait. Someplace with a Monet where you have to climb up to it. Monets are pretty stinking pretty."

"Oh, that's clever." Ginny's tone is straight up admiring. "Is it a helicopter tour? Private plane? Oh, wait." Ginny crinkles her forehead. "Famous flyer. Please tell me we don't have to go to Jersey to the Lindbergh monument."

Noah clasps his face. "No, not Jersey. Anywhere but Jersey."

Ginny laughs, and Noah nudges her, and all is right in their world.

Leo snaps his fingers. "Lindbergh. He's on a ceiling somewhere. There's a mural. Where is it, where the hell is it?"

"I know!" I crack the last clue.

We're off and flying faster than the famous pilot, en route to the Chrysler Building, seventy-seven floors high, boasting a mural of Lindbergh in the lobby ceiling. The building is arguably the most beautiful skyscraper in the city, and it's inarguably a masterpiece of the art deco movement. It's a gorgeous steel invitation to climb skyward and marvel at beauty, inside and out.

Once there, we torpedo through our tasks, confident we've made up for some of our lost time yesterday, and I'm hopeful we're in first place.

I don't want to win for me.

Or even for Leo.

I want to come out ahead for Ginny and Noah, these new friends who've brought me into the fold so easily, and for everyone else at Heavenly who gave me a chance.

Along the way back to Central Park, Ginny and Noah laugh and joke, teasing each other in a whole new way.

"You're really telling me you'd just lift your pizza?" He mimes eating a slice, flat as a board.

"That's how we do it down under."

"And I don't fold it when I visit my grandparents in Mexico City," Noah says, dropping into a Mexican accent for that line. "But we're New Yorkers now. We gotta fold it. That's how we do it here."

She laughs. "I assure you, the lift works just fine for a slice."

"Let me prove the fold is better. I'll take you out to get pizza and prove it."

"Fine. You can prove it."

He pumps a fist. "It's a date." He glances at her nervously. "It's a date, right?"

"It better be a date."

I smile at Leo, a few steps in front of me, and he smiles back. Yes, all is right in the world as we return to Strawberry Fields. Kingsley stands near a pack of ducks, tossing her sister's popcorn to the local waterfowl. Her sister pretends she's about to chuck chocolate at them. Kingsley grabs her arm before she can throw, then they laugh so loudly it carries to us.

I try to spot other teams, to figure out where we stand. As I scan the hillside, it looks like we're the second team to return.

I slow my pace when a familiar face comes into view.

My heart rate spikes.

I squint.

It can't be.

Am I seeing things?

Specifically, someone I haven't seen since my ex-husband's funeral.

She's toweringly tall, beautifully blonde, with carved cheekbones.

Pale-blue eyes somehow contain a sadness that will never be erased, alongside a strength I can't even imagine.

Tripp's mother.

31

LEO

I first met Vivian Lafferty when Tripp and I were juniors in college. We'd decided to get away from campus for the long weekend and spend it in Manhattan.

"My mom just remarried, and the new place is sweet. She's out of town with her husband. Let's crash there and get in trouble in the city."

"Maybe let's crash there, but not get in trouble in the city?"

"Fun police. I have a fake ID, and I intend to use it."

He did make good use of it, but everyone did in those days, so I thought nothing of it. And truthfully, there was nothing to it, though perhaps it was a harbinger. Besides, when Sunday morning rolled out and his mom returned, Tripp was sober, freshly shaven, and showered. Plus, she'd told him she was coming home early, so he surprised her and her new husband with Eggs Benedict, her favorite.

Over breakfast, she peppered me with questions,

wanting to know about my parents, my brothers, what I thought of school. By the time she'd finished, she issued a declaration. "I like you, Leo. You're a good influence on my hellion."

"Hellion? He's more like a hell-raiser." I'd winked, she'd laughed, and we'd proceeded to debate which was worse and which was better—a hellion or a hell-raiser. She was sold on me that day, and Tripp was sold on how well I got along with her.

At the wedding, I was his shield. "Keep my mom and dad apart. If my dad seems like he's going to make a dig—since that's his style—say something funny to cut the tension. Promise me?"

I kept that one, playing the referee he needed.

I was some kind of best man.

At the end of the night, Vivian thanked me. "I know it's not easy for him being around both of us. We're trying to be better. Well, I can only speak for myself. I'm trying to be better. I'm glad you were here for him."

That wasn't the first time she'd say those words to me—*I'm glad you were here for him.*

Now she's heading toward me, her lips turned up in a faint smile, a little rueful, as if she's done something a tiny bit wrong. "Leo. Look what I've resorted to. I have to track you down at work. You won't return my calls."

I laugh nervously, then wonder why the hell I'm laughing nervously.

Oh, right. Could it be because her former daughter-in-law spent last night in my arms?

That'd be the reason, and I swear I'm made of cellophane and she can see through me.

"Sorry about the phone tag."

Sorry about fucking my best friend's ex-wife.

"I'm just teasing." She drops a kiss to my cheek, her habit. "I actually called your office, and your assistant said you'd be here. I had an appointment nearby, so I thought I would pop over and find you." Her crystal eyes drift behind me, registering surprise. "And look who I found. Both of you."

Lulu appears by my side. "Hi, Vivian. It's so good to see you. You look amazing. Where did you get those jeans? And if you say on sale, I will bow down before you because those are incredible."

Vivian laughs. "You look fantastic too. I love your T-shirt—*Furious Napper*. Also, I paid full price."

"I feel better already." Lulu wipes her forehead dramatically.

"I haven't seen you since—" Vivian stops talking, stares at the sky. She collects herself, swallowing the words *the funeral*. "What have you been up to lately? I didn't expect to see you here too."

"Lulu's working with Heavenly," I answer, quickly explaining the situation, like I'd explain why my hand was in the secret chocolate stash as a kid.

"How fantastic. I'm thrilled everything is going well for you. I knew it would." Her graciousness is a sledgehammer aiming, unintentionally, for my lying heart.

"Thank you. It's a dream come true," Lulu says.

Vivian turns to me, clasping her hands. "I don't want to bother you in the middle of work, but I'm organizing a 10K and raising funds for addiction awareness and recovery. I was hoping you could get involved."

She hoists the hammer over her head.

"In what way?" I ask.

She lifts her chin, like she's trying so damn hard to stay strong. "Since one of the first 10Ks that you did was for this charity, I thought you could maybe say a few words at the start. Perhaps talk about your friendship. What Tripp meant to you. How things might have been different if awareness started earlier."

Hello, sledgehammer. Welcome to the glass case where the guilt statuette is stored inside me.

"Just to encourage the participants about what they're running for. Most have been touched by addiction in one way or another."

And the hammer comes down, smashing the glass into a thousand jagged shards.

I try to form words, but my tongue is made of cotton. I sneak a glance at Lulu, like maybe she can translate for me. But what can she say? Tripp's mom isn't making the request of her. She can't ask Lulu because Lulu's bond with her son broke before he died.

But mine?

The bonds between friends don't die when a person does. They last. Hell, I had dinner with him a few nights before he fell off the wagon again. He'd seemed so different that night at The Red Door.

My mouth is sawdust. "I'd be honored to."

"Thank you. It means a lot to me. It would have meant a lot to him."

She turns to Lulu, squeezing her arm. "I walked past your chocolate shop the other day, and I picked up a gift box for a friend. It made me so proud of you. I always wanted to see you become all you could be."

"Thank you for believing in me."

Vivian steps back, sighing softly. "It's good to see the

two of you again. It brings back memories. There were good ones, right? They weren't all bad?"

And now the sledgehammer goes for broke, smashing the shards to smithereens.

"Of course not. Most were good," I say.

"One of my favorites is when Tripp opened his restaurant and a few nights later, he invited all of us to celebrate. I wish I had a photo of that night. It had seemed then like all his dreams were coming true."

"Many did. You have to remember that," Lulu says, comforting her once again.

She stops when voices intensify, and suddenly the sound of people running grows louder. Laughter rains over Strawberry Fields. It's RaeLynn's team, and she rushes past then stops in her tracks.

* * *

RaeLynn stares at Vivian, studying her, then her icicle eyes sparkle like she's hit the jackpot. "Hi. Excuse me, but you look so familiar."

"I'm Vivian Lafferty."

"Are you . . . wait . . . you're Lulu's mother-in-law?" She gasps lightly. "Sorry, I meant former mother-in-law."

"Yes, that's me. But we still get along fine."

RaeLynn's smile expands. "I knew you looked familiar. This must be my lucky day. Lulu, I was friend-requesting you on Facebook last night and saw your wedding photo, and that's how I recognized your mother-in-law. *Former.*"

Lulu's brow pinches. "Wedding photos from eight years ago?"

RaeLynn laughs. "Facebook is so glitchy. They were the first ones to show up. Crazy, right?"

"That's not how Facebook works," I interject, but I have a sinking feeling it doesn't matter how the social network works. I have a feeling, too, that RaeLynn's bygones over the lost business pitch aren't gone at all.

Lulu jumps on the coming grenade. "Vivian, did you know that Bloomingdale's is having a sale? I've been dying to get my hands on some new Prada stuff. Want to cut out of here?"

Lulu doesn't wear Prada. Lulu doesn't shop at department stores.

"That sounds lovely."

But the look in RaeLynn's eyes tells me Lulu and I aren't winning. RaeLynn tees up her TNT. "You two should totally catch up, Lulu. I bet you have so much to talk about now that you're with Leo, the best man at your wedding."

There goes the dynamite.

Vivian's eyes flood with confusion. RaeLynn's truth bomb doesn't make sense. She turns to me for the truth. "You're together?"

"Yes."

Lying is pointless. She was bound to find out. Besides, Lulu and I are a good thing.

But as soon as that thought strikes me, another one does too. If I'm trying to convince myself that being with Lulu is okay—is it okay?

Vivian offers a conciliatory smile. "I'm happy for you."

But RaeLynn's not done. Her next words are a powder keg, and if I could give her Pretzelology on a platter right now, I would. "It's great when true love wins out after so many years, isn't it?" RaeLynn says with a happy sigh.

Lulu snaps her gaze to her. "What do you mean?"

"You guys are finally together. After all these years. Like it was meant to be from the start. I mean, did you ever really study those wedding photos closely?"

"Why?"

RaeLynn points to me, laughing ever so sweetly. "This guy? He's been in love with you since . . . What would you say, Leo? Since the wedding, for sure. But I'm betting, based on the way he looked at you in those photos, that it was well before then." The powder keg explodes. RaeLynn smiles gleefully, and she might as well rub her hands together and cackle. "Like I said, it's so wonderful when true love prevails after all this time."

Lulu's shocked expression is time-lapse photography, like she's flipping through the images of us in her mind. "Leo, is this true?"

"Oh, you didn't know?" RaeLynn's jaw drops dramatically. Briefly, I wonder how long she practiced that move last night while munching on popcorn and trawling through the bowels of Facebook.

But more importantly, I wonder if Lulu regrets some, most, or all of last night.

No matter what her answer is, my answer to her question remains the same.

"Yes."

32

LULU

What hits you in the chest but has no mass? What radiates in your bones but has no weight?

Shock.

My posture stiffens, and words tumble along my tongue. *How? When? What?*

But they're stuck behind the trapdoor of my mouth where I catch them all.

Suddenly, every moment with Leo over the last ten years flashes in my mind. The times we played Monopoly late into the night. The riddle book he gave me. The coffee before the intervention. The night Tripp had to work when I scored Lady Gaga tickets, and Leo said he'd come with me instead. The evening the three of us climbed the fence and pretended to be richie-rich folks in the city's exclusive Gramercy Park.

Did he scale the fence for me? Did he give me the riddle book because he was in love with me, or because we were friends? Does he even like Lady Gaga?

Vivian makes a show of looking at her watch,

smiling like all is right in the world, then says she has to take off for an appointment and it was great seeing us. She leaves. Ginny, Noah, and the rest of the scavenger hunt crew are still here nearby. They must have checked us back in for the challenge. But I can't focus on any of that.

"Let's talk about this privately," Leo says, and I nod catatonically then follow him to a bench on Central Park West, across from the famous building where John Lennon was shot.

I'm iconic and a legend lost his life outside me.

What is the Dakota?

But even riddles can't distract me from this strange new intel.

I face Leo. "Ten years?"

His eyes tell the truth, all vulnerability. "Since the day I met you."

Ground, meet jaw.

"Really?"

"I don't know if it was love then, but it was something. In class when we talked, I was captivated. You were captivating."

It feels like I've had amnesia and am waking up and learning who's my friend, who's my family, and who's not. "I was?"

"Completely. But then Tripp talked to you over lunch, and it was clear."

"What was clear?"

"You two had hit it off."

I don't recall falling for Tripp immediately. I didn't even think of him romantically until he asked me out. But as I try to cycle back to that fateful day, I suppose I can see that it came across that way. "And that was all it took?"

"That was all it took, Lulu. I fell for you that day, but I don't think it was love until a few months later. Not until the night you came over and brought chocolate and a bag of popcorn and we played Monopoly, and you were the most aggressive Monopoly player I'd ever encountered."

That night blinks in bright colors. "You liked that I took no prisoners in a board game?"

"You were ruthless, and you caught popcorn like a seal, and you made some chocolate squares with coconut, and you said, 'Try it.' And it was amazing, and I told you so."

"Were you just blowing smoke up my skirt?" The question is sarcastic, but there's confusion under it. Does this new wrinkle in our story change everything that came before it?

"No! I fucking meant it. I'm not a liar. But maybe you see me that way."

"No, I don't. I swear I don't." My voice sounds desperate, but I'm desperately trying to reenter the data of our friendship and process it anew.

"That was the night I knew I was in love with you, and I didn't know how to stop it."

My heart expands, and yet it turns the other way at the same time. It's wonderful and weird simultaneously to learn that his feelings started a decade ago, not a few weeks.

"Does this freak you out?"

I nod. "A little."

He takes my hand and squeezes. "I could give you a

million reasons, Lulu, but they all add up to this—love isn't rational. I don't even know that it's reasonable or makes any sense at all. You were vibrant and funny and daring. The more time we spent together, the deeper I fell. Your heart, your humor, your *you*-ness."

I want to fling my arms around him, smother him in kisses, and say, *Let's go home and revel in this*.

But it's also like watching a giraffe unzip his clothes and underneath he's really a . . . snow leopard.

Both are lovely creatures.

But the change takes some getting used to.

"I don't know what to say," I whisper, since Leo's not a giraffe anymore. "Do you even like Lady Gaga?"

"I do. Please don't tell anyone. Especially Dean." His crooked smile hooks into me, a momentary bit of levity.

"I won't say a word. I have a great . . . *poker face*."

His lips quirk up, and in that second, I feel we'll be fine.

Still, there is so much I want to understand. Because he does have a great poker face. Well, maybe not to RaeLynn, maybe not to someone determined to find the soft underbelly, but he bluffed with me for years. I understand why—self-preservation. But I don't entirely understand why he's never mentioned a word in the last few days.

"Why didn't you tell me last night?"

"You made it clear you wanted this all to be new."

"Were you going to tell me at all?"

"I wanted to."

"But you weren't sure exactly?"

He scrubs a hand over the back of his neck, staring at the Dakota, the scene of the crime many decades ago. "I was going to at some point. I just wanted us to go forward." He drops his head in his palms. "I didn't want it to come out like this."

"Did anyone else know?"

Lifting his face, he answers, "My mother suspected it, and she said something the day your mom came to her shop before her symposium. But we never talked about it in detail. Only Dean truly knows."

"Not Tripp's mom?"

He shakes his head.

"No one else?"

He raises his face and squeezes his eyes closed, and dread weaves through me. I know what's coming. I try to will it away. But it comes anyway when he opens his eyes. "Tripp."

The world becomes a wind tunnel sucking all the air from my lungs, from the sky. "Tripp knew?"

"He suspected. I never admitted it to him. But one night, he came over after you split and made me promise if I ever pursued something with you, I'd tell him first."

My jaw tics. Out of nowhere, a monsoon of fury swirls inside of me. "And did you? Did you promise him that?"

Leo swallows like there are nails in his throat. "He was relentless that night. And yes, he made me promise to tell him if I ever went for it with you."

"He *made* you?"

"And I'll never be able to honor it."

I shake my head, angry at him, angry at Tripp, angry at the freaking Dakota too. "It's not his goddamn choice."

"I know, but I still feel like shit that I can't say anything to him, whether he made me promise or not. Because that's the right thing to do—to give him a fucking heads-up. To tell my best friend, *Hey, I'm in love with your girl and I'm going to make a move*."

"I'm not his girl. It's not his choice." I tap my chest. Hard. "It's my choice who I get involved with. It's your choice who you get involved with. It's not *his* choice."

Leo's eyes brim with resignation. "Lulu, try to understand. He was my best friend."

"I've literally never been confused about that. I understand it completely, but you're acting like we're doing something wrong."

"I don't think we're doing something wrong." But his defeated voice says otherwise, and my heart hurts.

In this moment, Leo is a wrecked man.

He's not the man who made love to me last night.

He's not the man who held me close and whispered all his odes.

He's not the one who kissed me in front of a Klimt, who slipped me postcards, who ate birthday cake naked in my bed.

And in this moment, I don't care if he's a snow leopard or a giraffe. I don't care if he's loved me for years or for days. I'm fine with either option.

All I care about is that he's not all in.

And I am.

I'm so far in already.

My heart plummets to the sidewalk.

"I do understand," I whisper, my voice breaking.

"You do?" His rises with hopefulness.

"I understand completely. I'm clear on how you feel. I get that you're torn up."

He sighs with relief. "Thank you for understanding."

I square my shoulders, drawing a deep breath. "But right now, there's way too much of him in this relationship."

"What do you mean?"

"There are three of us in this, and there's only room for two. I was already married to him. And I don't want to be in a relationship with him again." I raise a hand and press it to Leo's chest, covering his heart. "I want to be in one with you. But right now? You're not all the way in."

His eyes implore me. "It's not always going to be like this, Lulu. His mom showed up and said those things, and then RaeLynn appeared and pulled out the carpet, and I have to process it. I have to process all I've done."

Sadness grips me, but so does certainty. "That's the thing—you seem to believe you've done something wrong. That *we're* something wrong."

"That came out wrong. I didn't mean it like that."

"But you're right."

"I am?"

"You are." I stare at him, my voice soft but firm. "I think processing is exactly what you need to do."

"What do you mean? What are you doing?"

I don't want to do this. But I have to. He's not ready, and I don't want a reluctant love. "I don't want half of you. I want all of you. I deserve all of you. I want you without resignation, without you looking over your shoulder. And I want you without him."

I look around. I'm not needed at the hunt. We finished the clue, we returned to the spot, and I'm free and clear.

I do one of the hardest things I've ever done.

I walk away from love.

33

LEO

That didn't exactly go as planned.

Then again, I didn't plan a damn thing. I simply hoped and clung to the edge of the boat in a battering sea.

Maybe not the best plan.

But I do have an ace up my sleeve—the last ten years of acting.

My poker face might not have been foolproof, but it's pretty damn good, and so is my immunity to her.

I do my damnedest to dial it all the way back up. I don't watch Lulu walk away. I don't linger on her silhouette as she heads south on Central Park West, blending into a slew of New Yorkers.

I know this drill. Been there, done that, have the jacket.

I'm a fucking pro.

I simply turn, head into the park, and rejoin the teams at Strawberry Fields, as if my life didn't just capsize courtesy of an overturned secret.

Ginny sees me and offers a sympathetic smile. I'm not sure how much she heard, or how much RaeLynn spewed to the crowd.

Nor do I care.

I shove my feelings down and make it through the end of the hunt, when I learn we finished in second place on today's challenge, and yesterday's last-place finish brought us down a notch overall. Kingsley and her sister announce the winning team.

News flash—it's not mine.

Finger-Licking Good is victorious, and George nearly leaps for joy when his name is announced.

I pat Ginny on the back then Noah too. "Better luck next time."

I go to the office and reacquaint myself with the familiar lineup of spreadsheets, contracts, deals, calls to return, calls to make, and conversations to have—conversations I drown myself in so I don't have to think of Lulu.

I refuse to think of Lulu.

All my years of training pay off.

I don't think of her at all.

* * *

By three in the afternoon, I'm leaning back in my chair, and I'm chuckling with a chocolate supplier over a meme he just showed me. For the record, cat memes are always funny.

Everything is fine here, thank you very much.

Just another day of normal.

Another day of *I'll get through this*.

As six in the evening draws near, there's a rap on my open door. Ginny pops in. "Hey, you."

"Hey."

"Call me crazy, but you look a little . . . how shall we say . . . like you've been sucking on lemons all day."

That sounds like a better way to spend the day than fighting off thoughts of the woman I love.

Wait.

I'm not thinking of her.

I pick up a pen and twirl it between my thumb and forefinger. "Nice to see you too."

She steps inside my office. "Are you bummed out about how the scavenger hunt ended? Because we'll live."

"No, I'm not. It's fine. It's whatever."

"'Whatever'? You're not a whatever person."

But maybe I should be. Maybe I should say *whatever* to this whole upturned mess, since I don't know how to fix it.

"I'm turning over a new leaf. Thinking of becoming a whatever person."

"Is this because of what happened in the park?"

I say nothing.

She shuts my door, moves some papers, and parks herself on the edge of my desk. "Listen, you didn't ask for my advice."

"I'm well aware of that."

"But I'm going to give it to you anyway."

"I had a feeling you would."

"The father of my child?"

I sit up. She never mentions him. Never talks about him. "Yeah?"

"He didn't get his act together when I told him I was pregnant."

"Okay."

"But now he wants to be in my kid's life. Now. When she's ten. And can you add up what that means?"

I'm good at math, but I have no clue how to perform Ginny's arithmetic. "No. I can't."

She pauses dramatically. "It means he missed ten years of her life."

"But Lulu's not pregnant."

"That's not the point."

"What is the point?"

"Do you want to miss ten years of *your* life?" Ginny leaves the question trailing behind her as she hops off my desk and squeezes my shoulder. "A bunch of us are going to this new place up the street that has pinball games. Let me know if you want to join us."

"I'll think about it."

But the more I think about it, the less I want to be with anyone tonight.

When moonlight blankets the city, I shut off the light in my office and leave, the last one to do so.

Once I'm home, the silence of my apartment cinches unwelcome arms around me. I try to pry them off, but it's powerful.

I'm not in the mood for silence.

I'm not in the mood for anything.

I turn to the walls in my home. "Fuck off."

I walk into the kitchen and talk to the counter, the fridge, the stove. "Fuck off."

I pivot around and pass the picture of Tripp and me at his restaurant. I stop to stare at it. Somehow, somewhere, I'm vaguely aware of words I could say to his image—thoughtful, caring words.

Those don't come. Others hiss from my lips.

"Most of all, fuck you."

But I don't think he's the one in the photo I'm speaking to.

34

LULU

My mother answers the door at eight that evening. I brandish a bag of Thai takeout, some popcorn, and my phone.

"I've got Facebook, and I'm not afraid to use it."

She laughs and lets me in. "I'll never forget how much you loved *Shrek* in middle school. You used a variation on that line for everything. 'I've got a dragon, and I'm not afraid to use it.'"

"It's your fault. You taught me how to study film and movies and pop culture."

"Correction: I taught you that *Shrek* was full of irony."

I frown, shouldering my way into her place. "My life is full of irony."

Once inside, I flop down in a chair at the table and extract the pad thai and pumpkin curry. She grabs forks and plates.

"Let's just eat straight from the carton."

"My home. My rules. Use plates."

"Fine."

She serves the food and slides a plate in front of me. "So . . ."

I sigh heavily. "You nailed it."

"Did I?"

"When you said years in his eyes. You were right."

"And that means what, exactly?"

I tell her everything. I've never held back from her. "And so, that's why I thought we could stalk my Facebook page, like that rhymes-with-witch did, and study every single photo ever to see if we see it too. I mean, this is what you're good at. Studying media."

With the forkful of noodles inches from her mouth, Mom shoots me a look. The look that says the cheese has slipped from the cracker. After she chews, she sets down the fork. "Let's not. Why don't we talk about it instead?"

I pinch the bridge of my nose. I don't want to talk about it. I do want to talk about it. But talking about it won't fix the bigger issue. I want the bigger issue fixed. I want him back. "It doesn't matter if he loved me for ten years or ten seconds. He's hung up on the past."

"Does it matter to you that he's felt this way for years? Does it change anything for you?"

A sob rattles up my throat, and I shake my head, answering with the whole truth. "No."

"Are you sure?"

I try to hold the tears at bay. "It doesn't. And honestly, I didn't stalk the photos. I didn't spend my afternoon staring at photo albums."

"What did you do?"

"I went to work. I made chocolate. I fiddled with

recipes. I served customers. And I missed him. It's stupid because it's only been one day, maybe two, that I realized I felt this way. And I don't get it, Mom. Why do I miss him this intensely? It's only been a few hours since I saw him. Well, it's been nine hours, thirty-three minutes, and twenty-seven seconds since I told him to figure it out. And I miss him like it's been years."

She fights off a grin. "Nine hours, thirty-three minutes, and twenty-seven seconds?"

"Give or take on the seconds."

She laughs. "You miss him because you fell in love with him. You miss him because you want his love in return. He's loved you for years; you've loved him for a few days. But to both of you it feels like years. Think about that."

I absorb her words, trying to absorb her meaning. But all I know is I long for him. Maybe this is how he felt for me all the time. That awareness makes my heart ache harder.

"The thing is, I *should* be scared that he's felt this way for a long time. I *should* want to go look at every photo, analyze every conversation, and study every e-mail. And I did feel that way for a while. For an hour, maybe."

"My my, you have become the most efficient woman at processing your emotions."

I laugh lightly. "I think I have. I think that's what I learned from my marriage. How to navigate through the storm. How to see when there wasn't starlight to guide me. But I don't need to pore over the past. I've done that. I've spent enough time on it. All I want is my future. And I can't have it yet. I can't have it unless Leo decides to navigate through *his* stuff."

Mom reaches for my hand. "The waiting is the hardest part."

"How long do I wait?"

"How much do you love him?"

"As much as I loved my tiara when I was nine. As much as I loved the twenty-five-thousand times I listened to Christina Aguilera in high school and drove you crazy, even though you'd never have admitted that out loud. And maybe, sometimes, more than chocolate. So what do I do?"

She laughs. "You think I'm going to tell you what to do?"

"Please. Just tell me. For once in your life."

She shakes her head and crosses her arms. "Not gonna do it."

I grab her arms, trying to uncross them. "Pretty please with multimedia analysis and popular culture discourse on top."

Her laughter bursts across her apartment. "Lulu, just be yourself. Wait for him. Or don't wait for him. Speak your mind. Or don't speak your mind. Tell him what's in your heart. Or don't tell him. Mostly, *you do you*. Because you?" She cups my cheek. "You are fabulous just the way you are. You are on the other side. And whatever you do, you're going to be just fine."

She's right.

I am going to be fine.

Maybe even better than fine. I can't do a damn thing about his issues. But I can do something about how I feel.

After we finish the Thai food, I grab my phone.

But I don't stalk wedding photos on Facebook or elsewhere.

I text Cameron and Mariana, and I ask if they're free this weekend.

Then as Mom and I watch *Shrek 2*, pointing out the clever way the script both subverts and embraces fairy tales, I compose a letter in my head to Leo.

I make plans to send it to him tomorrow.

35

LEO

I swing at the white ball the next morning.

It whizzes past me.

Another white orb flies in my direction.

With laser focus, I keep my eye on the ball and take aim as it sails over the plate. I connect in a satisfying *thwack*. The ball goes sailing all the way to the fence, smacking the chain link at the edge of the batting cages.

I'm here because there's no cemetery to go to. There are no graveside conversations to be had, like in the movies. Besides, graveside conversations are stupid. A rotting pile of bones can't exonerate you.

But something has to.

Something has to give.

I've tried running all night.

I've tried furniture stripping all morning.

The way I see it is this—the busier I can make myself, the better I can process and the sooner I can be with Lulu.

If I push this boulder of the past higher up the hill, soon I'll reach the top. And maybe it won't come sliding back down to crush me.

I zero in on another ball, whacking it to kingdom come.

Yes. That's it. More imaginary home runs. More time in the cage. More *anything*. I grit my teeth, willing myself to figure this out.

"You know, it's not about him."

I startle, and the next ball flies past me, landing with a *thunk* at my feet. I swivel around to find Dean outside the batting cage, and I turn off the machine. "What are you doing here?"

"When I texted you this morning, you said you were going to the cages. A little slow on the uptake today, mate? Did you take one to the head?"

"I mean, why did you come?"

"It's so nice to see you too."

"I'm sorry. I'm a fucking mess."

"I know." He looks me over. Dean knows the basic details of what went down at the end of the hunt. I don't keep secrets from Dean. "Leo, it's not about him."

"Yeah?"

"It's not about him. It's about you. That's what I came here to tell you. Because I had a feeling you were going to try to run your feelings away, strip them away, South American history them away. Am I getting warmer?"

I gulp. More like red-hot. I leave the cage, joining him on the other side of it. "Very warm."

"Or perhaps whack them away."

"It's not working."

"Shocking."

"So, what do I do?"

He laughs. "You're the man who always talks about choices. Why don't you make a choice to move the fuck on?"

"Gee. Why didn't I think of that?"

"It's not about thinking it. It's about *doing* it." He claps me on the back. "The present is a gift. Start acting like it. Otherwise, you're going to be spending a lot of days and nights at the batting cage."

That's all he says. That's the only advice he drops on me. But it starts to wiggle around in my head, making its way to my heart.

"Want to go a round?" I ask.

He points to the ball machine. "Come to think of it, I do. And I believe the next round, and the one after that, and the next—they're all on you."

He grabs a helmet from the ground, drops it on his head, walks into the cage, and proceeds to whack the hell out of baseballs for the next few minutes. He has cannons for arms. It's insane, and as he nabs hit after hit, something loosens inside me.

Something I didn't realize was coiled too tight.

A sadness I barely knew I had.

I lost my best friend, and that stung.

But I've gained something else along the way.

Another one.

This guy. Right here. He's part of my present, part of my life, and I want to enjoy this time. He's not the same kind of friend as Tripp. He doesn't have to be.

Dean's himself, and I can be myself with him.

As soon as that thought occurs to me, I let go of a little more of the guilt I'd been holding on to.

I wasn't always myself with Tripp. I was holding a big secret inside.

But with Dean, I can be myself.

And even though I definitely don't want to spend my nights here at the cages, right now I'm sure this is exactly where I'm supposed to be.

When Dean's done, I take my turn, and like that, we spend an hour or so at the batting cages, and it's the most fun I've had with a buddy in ages.

It's fun, and it's freeing, and when I return home, I'm ready to tackle what to do next.

Then, when I unlock the door to my apartment, I find a letter on the floor.

36

LULU

Mariana is parked at the curb outside my apartment, Jackie O glasses on, her thick dark hair swept back in a black scarf with white polka dots, '50s movie star. Cameron stretches his long legs in the passenger seat, shades on, tapping out a drumbeat to the rhythm of Tom Petty's "American Girl" on the shiny car door.

With my weekend bag slung over my shoulder, I rush down the steps to the . . . brand-new red convertible. Holy sexy automobile. "Where did you get this little slice of heaven?"

"I won my last case," Mariana says with a twinkle in her eyes. "So I treated myself."

Cameron raises a palm to high-five her. "It's one helluva treat. And it's good to be a lawyer."

She blows on her pewter-colored nails, perfectly polished. "Billable hours for the win, my friends. That's what it's all about."

Cameron points his thumb at her. "This is the kind

of woman who needs a pantsuit. Someone who charges four hundred dollars an hour."

She pats his shoulder. "You're cute. Four hundred an hour? Who do you think you're dealing with?"

"Oh, excuse me, Mrs. Esquire."

She taps his head, as if she's bonking him. "Five hundred fifty dollars. Talk about them apples."

I hop into the back seat of the sweet sports car. "God bless Yale Law School graduates."

"You know it."

Cameron cranes his head around. "All right, my pretty ladies, let's hit the road before I wrestle away the wheel. You do know sports cars are my temptation. I nearly bought a Ferrari at a car auction in Miami."

Mariana lowers her shades to stare at him. "You *nearly* bought a Ferrari? How does one *nearly* buy a Ferrari?"

"I thought about it a lot. Dreamed about it. Fantasized about it too."

"That is not nearly buying a Ferrari," Mariana corrects.

"Besides, I thought you were dreaming about your mystery woman in Miami," I tease. "Maybe you'll tell us."

He chuckles deeply. "Maybe I will. For now, Lulu, turn your phone off for the weekend."

I make a show of hitting the power off button. They clap their approval, then Mariana leans a little closer to Cameron, their shoulders nearly touching. "If you're good to me, I'll let you drive once we're in the Hamptons."

"Please, go on. Define *good to you*."

"No bitching about my driving is what's good to me."

"I would never do that. Also, have I mentioned what great taste you have in music?"

"Oh, you are smart." Mariana turns the engine on and checks her mirrors. "All systems go for a weekend getaway. We need to make this girl un-sad."

A pinch of sadness fills my eyes as I kiss her cheek then his. "You guys are the best."

And they are—as soon as I told them I needed to escape for the weekend, Cameron booked a beach rental in the Hamptons, and Mariana offered to drive. That's what friends are for.

A lump rises in my throat as she pulls into traffic. It's a knot of emotion for my friends.

For the foundation of my new life in New York.

My starting over.

But before we leave the city, there's one thing I need to do.

I tap Mariana's shoulder before she cranks the music too loud. "Can we make a pit stop first?"

"We're not stopping for H&H bagels. It's hell there on a Saturday morning."

Cameron rubs his belly. "H&H bagels are the bomb, Mariana. Right along with Puccini."

As she slows at a light, he grabs his phone, suddenly transfixed by a message, I presume.

Mariana glances at me in the rearview mirror. "Looks like someone has a little online lover."

He doesn't respond, simply taps away with a goofy grin on his face.

"And who is making you smile like that? Is this grandma or your real mystery woman?" I ask.

He looks up, a glint in his eyes. "Perhaps it's the real one."

"Are you ever going to tell us about her?"

"Maybe I'm saving the story for the beach."

"My ears are waiting," I say, then tell Mariana where to make the pit stop.

Last night I wrote a letter to Leo. It's safely tucked in my purse. A few minutes later, Mariana pulls up to Leo's building, and I ask the doorman to let me leave the letter under Leo's door. He obliges.

Afterward, I scurry back to the car, and we cruise along the highway out to the Hamptons, singing to Mariana's road-trip mix—Def Leppard's "Photograph," The Eagles' "Life in the Fast Lane," Rihanna's "Shut Up and Drive"—singing until we're hoarse, until our voices are shot, and then singing some more.

Then we make up words when Mariana finds some Puccini to blast.

The music isn't enough to make me stop missing Leo. It's not enough to make me stop loving him. But singing songs at the top of my lungs with my two closest friends is enough to remind me what I have here in New York.

I have my family, I have my home, I have my shop, and I have my friends.

I'd really like to add Leo to the mix, but right now, with the sun shining brightly, the road unfurling, and the beach mere miles away, I'd say four out of five isn't too bad.

I close my eyes and imagine Leo opening the letter.

Well, it's actually a postcard. A picture of Roy Lichtenstein's *The Kiss.*

Dear Leo,

You asked if you were freaking me out. Let me assure you— I'm not freaked out in the least. Nor am I analyzing every little thing that has happened over the years. I think love is a gift, whether it comes quickly or has been burning across time.

I didn't expect to fall for you. I didn't think I'd feel this way, and I certainly never set out for us to happen. But we happened. And I do love you. I feel the love completely, in a wildly hopeful, incandescently happy way.

I suppose some things don't change. I believe in the poetry of love, and I believe in hope.

I hope madly that you'll see me the way I see myself— I'm not anyone's girl. I'm my girl.

And I want to be yours, fully and without reservation.

That's the only way.

Love,
Lulu

37

LEO

I'm not worthy.

As I turn the card over, staring at the bright blue, red, and yellow of the comic book couple, I know with a cold, stark certainty that I'm definitely not worthy of her.

But so what?

The woman wants me.

The woman loves me.

And I'd be a fool to throw this away.

I'd be an absolute idiot to take any longer to process anything at all in the world.

What kind of man walks away from this kind of love?

A stupid one.

I might be stubborn, I might be tortured now and then, and I am definitely, absolutely pigheaded.

But stupid? I am not.

I fold the card, tuck it into my wallet, and vow to

keep it with me always. I don't know what to say to her, and I still don't know that I completely feel like this is okay. But at least I don't feel that guilt. At least now I'm free of that.

I grab my phone and call Lulu.

It goes straight to voice mail.

I do it again.

Same response.

I flop down on the couch, read the note again, letting her words fill me with champagne happiness. Because that's what this is.

The trouble is, I don't want to sit here. I need to keep busy while I wait for her to call back. But I don't want to run, or hit baseballs, or work on furniture.

I have business to tend to. Personal business. There's someone I need to apologize to.

I find Vivian's number and call her. She answers immediately, and I ask if I can come see her. She tells me I'm always welcome at her home.

Maybe I always will be, and perhaps that's simply a good thing, not a thing to feel guilty about. In fact, it's a great thing that I forged a friendship worthy of admiration and respect from a mother.

I pat my pockets to make sure I have my phone, keys, and wallet, when my gaze catches on that photograph of Tripp and me. I stare at it, seeing it in a new light, remembering that night.

Mesmerized, I step closer, like I've turned a flashlight on the faded edges of my memory.

That wasn't just some night at his restaurant.

That was the night he opened it.

And I'd completely forgotten how special that night was to someone—someone who's still here.

I grab the picture frame and catch a Lyft across town.

* * *

Vivian clutches the photo to her chest. "This I will cherish. This is something I wanted so badly. Thank you."

"It's the least I can do."

"No. It's the most. I think of that night fondly. He was the happiest he'd ever been. That's my memory. That's what I choose to hold on to. Not the other stuff. Not the terrible things. But this night." She taps the glass for emphasis.

"How did you get there?"

"Get where?"

"To this place. To your clarity. To embracing only the good."

She laughs, the wise kind of laugh only a woman who's been through hell can have. "Sit. I'll make some tea." She stage-whispers, "Tea's the only acceptable drink for a serious conversation."

She makes some, then we sit and drink and talk about funny moments, the little jokes, the times we all laughed over the years. We debate hellions and hell-raisers, and we decide Tripp was simply both.

It's cathartic—a catharsis I needed.

"Vivian, I wanted to apologize."

"Whatever for?"

"For yesterday. For the way the news all came out."

She waves a hand, seeming to make it all go away. "Please."

"No, I mean it. I didn't want any of it to come out that way, and I'm sorry you had to walk into that mess."

"Don't think twice about it."

"Can I ask you something?"

"You know you can."

"What did you think when you heard I was with Lulu?"

She smiles faintly. "I was shocked at first, but then I wasn't. I always liked her. I always liked you. The two of you liked Tripp. You all had so much in common, and I suppose it's not a surprise that you'd wind up together. Maybe it was inevitable. Some people are simply drawn to each other. They're magnets, and they can't stay away." She takes a drink of her tea. "You and Lulu are magnets. How is it going?"

I wince. "That's the thing. It's not going right now. She told me to figure out my stuff."

"Ouch."

"I deserved it. I've been tangled up in guilt."

"Oh, sweetheart. Do you really think Tripp wouldn't want you to be happy?"

"I don't know."

She stares sharply at me, her ice-blue eyes challenging. "Think, Leo, think."

"I've been thinking. It's all I've been doing. And every time I think about it, I keep looking for permission."

"How's that working out for you?"

I laugh wryly. "Not so well."

"I'm not surprised."

"What do I do now? I'm waiting for Lulu to call me back, but I don't even know what to say. What do I say to prove I'm not reluctant?"

"Do you want to be with her, no questions asked?"

"I love her so much it hurts. I love her so much it feels incredible. I love her so much, I don't want to give her up. I love her so much, I would give her up if I had to. But I don't want to. All I want is to move forward the way she wants. I want to be okay moving forward."

Her brow furrows, as if she's considering all I've said. "Did you come to me for permission? Like I'm a proxy for him?"

"No." But maybe in some way I did. "Maybe?"

"Look at me."

I meet her eyes.

"I'm not going to give it to you. Because you're not going to find that, and somehow you're going to have to be okay with it. Because you know what? I'm not the one to give you permission, and he's not either." She taps my heart. "This is where it comes from."

The earth stops on its axis. The oceans cease churning. In that moment, I realize how completely wrong I've been. I've been looking for permission in the wrong place.

It exists in only one place, and that's inside of me.

I have to give it to myself.

* * *

I say goodbye to Vivian, thanking her profusely. I walk

across Central Park, remembering the laughter, the friendship, the needling, the teasing, the calls to go out and celebrate, the calls to go to sporting events, the calls to go help each other move a piece of furniture, test out a recipe, anything, everything.

And then the last call. The night we went to The Red Door, the hottest eatery in town.

He can't call me anymore and tell me that everything is cool and to just go for it with the woman of my dreams.

And finally, I don't want that anymore. I don't need it any longer. Because I'm giving it to myself.

I'm the only one who can decide to love Lulu the way she deserves. With my whole heart. I'm the only one who can go forward gladly, exuberantly, without a shred of reluctance.

Life is full of choices, and I'm making this choice.

It's exhilarating.

Tonight, I say goodbye to guilt.

I shout *see you later* to any last doubts.

I call out *I'm done* to the past.

The choice is now, and it's high time to embrace the present and make room for the future—an absolutely fantastic future with the woman I adore.

The woman who's somehow wonderfully, fantastically mine.

Well, as long as I don't fuck things up anymore.

Shoot.

I need to fix things, stat.

That's when I start running.

There's not a moment to waste.

I run out of the park, down Fifth Avenue toward my

home, dialing and dialing, reaching voice mail every time.

But voice mail won't win.

I'm a resourceful man. I strike business deals for a living. I know how to work my way around a problem.

I call her best friend, and he answers.

38

TRIPP

Nearly two years ago, The Red Door restaurant

I raced up the stairwell to Leo's apartment, taking the steps two by two, not bothering with the elevator.

I had to get his ass in gear.

I reached the fifth floor, sprinted down the hall, and banged on the door.

A few seconds later, he yanked it open. "I told you I'd be downstairs in five," Leo said. "Is your watch broken?"

"I don't wear a watch."

"No kidding."

"We gotta go. I'm telling you. *Now.* Time's a-wasting."

He laughed. "Like the restaurant won't hold the reservation for you?"

I rolled my eyes. "That's not the point. The point is I

got us into The Red Door, and now I don't want to wait. C'mon."

I'd snagged a table at the hippest new spot in all of Manhattan. This place was so cool, and I was sure it would inspire a whole new spate of dishes at my restaurant. Lord knew, I needed the help.

Not to mention, I needed some dough to pay the overdue bills.

But I wasn't going to worry about that tonight.

There would be time to worry.

For now, it was Leo and Tripp hanging out, eating the best food, and living the single life in New York City.

A few minutes later, Leo shut the door behind him, and we took off for the restaurant.

Soon we were dining on bacon-wrapped shrimp, succulent butternut squash ravioli, and mushroom truffles, and I was in heaven. "This is so good. Why don't I have this on the menu at my place?"

He laughed as he took another bite of the mushrooms. "Because you'd be stealing another chef's dishes?"

I waved a hand dismissively. "Who cares? I need truffles on the menu. And I need them now." I banged a fist on the oak table.

"Do it, then, man. Just do it." He lifted a glass of iced tea and offered it to clink with mine.

My iced tea.

I tapped my glass. "See? I'm a good boy."

"Keep it up, man. Keep it up."

"I will. I absolutely one-hundred-percent promise that I will."

I could turn over a new leaf. Tonight, I was going to start over. I hadn't had a drop in a few weeks. I was trying. I would keep trying. This was the beginning of a new life.

And hell, in this new life, Leo could be with Lulu. I could see them together. I knew he was in love with her, even though he denied it that one time I brought it up. I needed to tell him that promise was dumb. She wasn't mine. She hadn't been in a long, long time.

He didn't need my permission. Didn't need my blessing. I wanted him to be happy. Hell, he was the best friend I'd ever had, and he should have the world.

"So, that woman I met recently? Amy?"

I nodded. He'd mentioned her a few times. "The one you wanted to ask out?"

"I started seeing her. She's pretty cool."

I sat back and listened as he told me about a new woman.

Some other night I'd bring up Lulu, just in case things didn't work out with Amy. My buddy would end up with Lulu. I was sure of it.

After all, there'd be time.

There was always time.

39

LULU

A sound whispers across the tiled floor, a kind of *whoosh*.

I blink open my eyes, figuring it's the wind from the ocean. We left the windows open, and my room is closest to the beach.

I sit up. "Cameron? Mariana?"

No one answers, and my skin prickles. This is that moment when girls do something stupid in a horror movie.

"Cameron?"

I call his name louder then flick on the lamp by my bed.

Is that a postcard on the floor?

A dash of hope flutters in my chest. I fling the covers away, and I am that girl in a horror movie.

Only I'm not.

Because this is a different story. It's a story where the girl chases a Chagall.

I get out of bed, kneel, and pick up the postcard.

It's an image of the artist's *L'anniversaire*, a gorgeous, dreamy painting of two lovers floating above the floor, kissing, enrapt.

The painting Leo said he'd get me next time.

My heart thunders in my chest, wild mustangs stampeding across the earth. *Please let next time be now.*

I turn it over.

"Next time, I'll give you a Chagall." That's what I told you, and I meant it. And I hope you'll forgive me.

For what?

I open the door and find a trail of Chagalls across the living room floor, postcard after postcard. I pick up the next one.

I love you.

The next one.

It's always been you.

And another, as my heart starts to glow.

I tried to stop loving you. I think I succeeded for a while. But you're you, and you're wonderful, and I fell in love with you all over again.

One more.

And this time? It's better. Because I didn't fall alone. I fell with you.

Tears slip down my face as I grab the next card, following the trail.

I fell madly, joyfully, enthusiastically in love with you, as you fell for me.

I grab the next one as the glow spreads from my chest all the way through me.

I still can't believe I'm writing this. I can't quite fathom that I'm not experiencing this solo. Have I mentioned it's so much better to love you when you love me back?

"I bet it is," I whisper, grabbing one more.

I don't think I can compare the two. Loving you from afar was painful and exquisitely torturous. Loving you near is wonderful and exquisitely blissful.

A smile commandeers my face. My whole being. I'm almost at the deck, where a night breeze blows and stars light the sky.

I pick up the last one.

This is new love. I love who you are now. I love your spirit, and your humor, and your wild ideas, and I love your endless, beautiful heart and your profound capacity to love.

I love that you want this.

I love that you want us.

I want it all too.

My face is awash with tears as I stand, peering out onto the deck. A sliver of moonlight shines on the wood. Leo steps out of the shadows from the beach, his brown eyes brimming with hope.

"I'll give you all the kisses in the world, all the paintings in the world. I'll give you all my love. Always. Will you have me?"

No question has ever been easier to answer. I'm exploding with light and joy and all the love I've ever wanted. I launch myself at him, throwing my arms around his neck, kissing him madly as I say over and over *yes, yes, yes.*

I don't need to quiz him.

I don't need to know how he's arrived at this conclusion.

I don't need the details of how he processed things.

Because he did.

Because he's here.

And because he kisses me with all his heart, his mind, and his body.

There are no more questions. There is no more past.

We kiss under the moon and the stars until kisses turn into fervent gasps and needy touches. I pull him inside, take him to my room, and show him that I love him heart, mind, and body.

When we're done, I run my fingers down his chest.

"How did you find me?"

He smiles playfully. "You have very good friends."

I smile too. "I do. I have everything."

He takes my hand, links his fingers through mine, and squeezes. "So do I."

LULU

One month later

"What breaks and never falls, and what falls and never breaks?"

Leo peers at the ceiling of the train as it rumbles into Grand Central, chugging to a stop. We've spent the weekend in Connecticut at a quaint bed and breakfast. He reaches for my hand, slings my bag over his shoulder, then, with a proud glint in his eyes, announces, "Day . . . and night."

I plant a congratulatory kiss on his cheek. "You're so smart. Have I ever told you how smart you are? Have I ever told you how sexy that is?"

He taps his chin. "I'm not sure you have. But please, feel free to go on and on about all of those attributes."

"You're smart, sexy, devoted, great company, good with opening jars, excellent at reaching the top shelf, and incredibly good at taking the trash out. Which makes you a dream man."

"Wait till you see how I can hang a new shower curtain."

I fan my face as we walk off the train then stroll through the terminal. "That might be too much."

"I'll do it when you're not home, then."

Home.

I'm home when I'm with him. And home is where we'll live together.

I'm moving in with him in a few weeks. His place is bigger, which translates into more room for colorful throws and pillows. Plus, his state-of-the-art kitchen is orgasm-inducing to this chocolatier who loves to experiment with recipes late at night.

Another benefit? His building is dog-friendly, so I've started fostering small pups with a local rescue. So far, we've offered a temporary home to Edward, Ferdinand, and a crazy chihuahua named Snapdragon, and they've already found their fur-ever homes too.

I love being home with Leo, but we also try to escape from the city as much as we can, when we're not fostering pups.

Now, we make our way through the station, drinking in the familiar sights from the scavenger hunt, like the constellations above us. "It's kind of funny. Being in this train station that second day of the hunt made me realize it was time to go for it with you. All those clues from the past helped me see I wanted a chance with you."

He gazes upward at the stars and planets. "I'd like to thank the Academy and Grand Central Terminal. Also,

Kingsley for organizing the scavenger hunt. And the chocolate fountain that made Lulu practically take off her clothes way back when. Also, thank you, llama panties."

I laugh and dot a kiss to his forehead.

* * *

That afternoon, we head to Bryant Park for a quick get-together to celebrate the scavenger hunt and give out trophies, since we never really had a proper finale last month. We stroll in front of the New York Public Library on Library Way—the sidewalk lined with plaques inscribed with quotes from great works of literature.

I point to one from Willa Cather's *O Pioneers!* and Leo reads it aloud: "'There are only two or three human stories, and they go on repeating themselves as fiercely as if they had never happened before.'"

I clasp Leo's hand more tightly. "I love that. This would be a good riddle for a hunt. You can say something along the lines of 'What's familiar, but also new every time you open it? You'll find me looking down, among so many others, each one hinting at a different story.' And the answer would be Library Way."

"Have I told you how sexy and smart you are?"

"Why, yes, shower me with compliments. They'll get you everywhere."

He squeezes my ass and growls in my ear. "Exactly where I want to be."

Inside the park, we spot Ginny and Noah holding

hands. As we walk past them, they're debating whether cones are better than cups.

"See, when you get ice cream in a cone, there's absolutely no waste. You don't have to throw a thing out," he says.

"Right, but when you get it in a cup, it's pure. It's just ice cream. You don't have a cone to sully the taste."

"How on earth does a cone sully the taste? It makes it even better."

"Maybe I want my ice cream all to itself, just like I want my man."

He sidles up against her, doing his full sexy Latino accent. "You can definitely have me all to yourself. Anytime, anywhere."

"Have I ever mentioned your accent is hella sexy?" Ginny says to him.

"I knew it! Also, so is yours. Like, the hottest in all the world."

I look at them, then at Leo, whispering, "True love born from true arguers. That's definitely the two of them."

I survey the scene, cataloging the others from the hunt—minus RaeLynn, since I presume she's descended to her secret lair to plot more nefarious misdeeds. My heart scampers away from me when I see three adorable redhead babies in a triple-wide stroller and one very happy dad pushing them toward us. George's skin is a little more golden than it was last time, and his eyes sparkle. He traveled to the Bahamas and donated the ten thousand dollars in prize money to an organization that provides school supplies for low-income children. He's officially all kinds of awesome.

I wave to him and rush over, bending to dote on the babies. "They're so cute. I'm overloading on the adorable. How do you even stand it every day?"

"It is their cuteness indeed that gets me through. Also, a vacation helped." He holds out his arms. "How do I look? Like the most relaxed man in the universe? Tanned, rested, and . . . well, ready for another vacation."

"You look like the guy who deserved a vacation and made one hell of a good use of it."

"Determination was the name of the game. That was all. I saw the prize, and I said, 'I absolutely must have it, no matter what.'"

"I'm glad you won. Every now and then, someone who deserves a prize wins a prize."

A few minutes later, Kingsley clears her throat to say it's time to present the trophy to the victor, but one of George's little girls cries before Kingsley can hand over the statue. Another baby joins the chorus. I scoop up crying baby number one, and before I know it, Leo is by my side helping with the other.

The sight of him holding a little one in his arms is almost too much for me to bear. My ovaries huddle and plan a strategy to tackle Leo and demand attention RIGHT NOW. "Forget everything I said earlier. This is the sexiest you've ever been."

"Is that so?"

"Yes, and I want one of these for my own."

"You're suggesting we take one of George's babies?"

The father of three jumps into the conversation as he tends to the third baby. "Anytime you two want to babysit, you know where to find me. In fact, how about five o'clock today? I'll pay you double."

I lean in to stage-whisper. "Confession: you don't have to pay me a dime."

"You mean you'll pay me? Even better."

"Name the date and time, and I'm there."

"I knew I liked you. If you ever need a chocolate fountain, I'm your man."

Leo smiles as he interjects, "So you want one of those?"

"A chocolate fountain? Yes. I do. I told you I like them."

"A baby, Lulu."

"Um, yeah. How could you tell?" The funny thing is, I'm not worried that my baby fever is going to scare him off. Leo's not easily spooked. He's also ridiculously good with babies.

He nuzzles the redhead in his arms and whispers something in a sweet baby language, then he looks over at me. "Then I better get you something first."

* * *

A few days later, Leo tells me a book he requested on antique furniture styles has arrived, and asks if I want to join him to fetch it.

I do, so we head to the New York Public Library and wander through the stacks, sniffing old books and playing a game to see who can find the most absurd history book. He wins when he locates a tome on poison in the court of James I.

We leave on a mission for lunch, scamper down the

steps, and wander along Library Way, reading the quotes from the plaques. He gestures to the Willa Cather one, a few feet away.

"Hey, Lulu. What's made of stone, contains a quote from an American author, and says something profound about stories?"

Seriously? "Are you soft-balling me?"

His brown eyes twinkle with mischief. "Maybe I am."

I swivel around and point to the ground. "It's that plaque. That's the answer to your supremely easy riddle."

He shakes his head, satisfaction spreading across his face. "No. The answer is where I'm going to ask you to make me the happiest man in the world."

I gasp as he drops down to one knee on the Willa Cather plaque, reaches for a royal-blue velvet box from his pocket, and flips it open. "Lulu Diamond, will you marry me?"

My heart executes backflips. "Yes! A million times, yes."

I hold out my hand, and he slides a ring on my finger as tears rain from my eyes. He stands, takes me in his arms, and kisses me in front of Manhattan, in front of the whole world, with a breathlessness and hope that makes me feel like we could be on a postcard.

* * *

A few months later, I take George up on his chocolate fountain offer, much to the consternation of my husband-to-be.

Leo protests till he's blue in the face.

It's messy. It's gross. It's a vat of germs.

My response? *It's fun.*

We compromise and order one for our rehearsal dinner, instead of the wedding.

Confession: it *is* messy. But it's a blast as I pop strawberries onto skewers and dip them. Cameron willingly plays the role of fountain police, and he and Mariana make excellent sergeants, ensuring no one dips in a finger or a face.

That's not the only chocolate at the festivities. We also give away our new chocolate collection to all our guests. I'm thrilled with how the Rising Star collection turned out. We call it Kissed by Chocolate, and the chocolates are packaged in art deco wrappers of stylized kiss paintings, with constellations of stars printed on the inside. They also outsold Frodo's chips last quarter, and Kissed by Chocolate tops all the Heavenly lines too.

Seems, in our own way, that we won the team-building competition after all.

Our wedding the next day is a simple affair. Leo's parents are here, along with his brothers, my mother and her boyfriend, Cameron and his mystery woman, Mariana, Dean and Fitzgerald, George, his wife and the babies, Kingsley and her husband, and Ginny and Noah, who are inseparable and next in line for vows, thanks to the ring Noah gave her last month.

Tripp's mom is here too, and that means a lot to me.

My mother doesn't give me away this time. I'm my own person, with my own dreams, my own goals, and I don't belong to anyone else. That's why this marriage will be different than my first.

Because Leo and I are sturdier than a three-legged stool. We're a pair, the kind whose bonds don't break. Sometimes life gives you a second chance at love, and if you're lucky enough to spot it and wise enough to seize it, you better be strong enough to keep it.

I am.

We are.

And we will be.

EPILOGUE

Leo

A week later

A tropical breeze blows through the open shutters. Stretching, I swing my legs off the bed.

The morning sun of my Costa Rican honeymoon floods the suite. My wife's not here. She left a note that she was out for a morning walk.

I head to the bathroom, brush my teeth, run a hand through my hair, then meander to the deck to enjoy the sun and the coconut-scented air that reminds me of her.

Then again, nearly everything reminds me of her, but the reminders no longer hurt. They don't mock me with what I can't have. They're a promise of all that I'm so lucky to call my own.

I pop in an audiobook and get lost in the modern

history of this country. A few minutes later, the door snicks open, and I remove my earbuds.

"Morning, handsome."

Lulu's wild hair is even wilder here, framing her beautiful face. She waggles a white paper bag. "Rice and beans, flan, some mangoes, and I have coffee too."

She sets the breakfast on the table on the deck, as the sun hoists itself higher over the ocean.

"Good morning to you too."

"Oh, I also found this with the breakfast."

She hands me a postcard of a couple kissing on the beach. Probably something she picked up at a local souvenir shop. "What's this for?"

"Why don't you take a look?"

I flip it over to find her handwriting.

My eyes widen, and my skin prickles with excitement chased by hope. "For real?"

Her smile touches my soul as she whispers, "For real."

I cup her cheeks and kiss her, then read her words aloud. They're the best words she's ever written to me, and that's saying something.

"*What's a little bit of you, a little bit of me, still all new, and arrives in a birthday suit?*"

THE END

Want to know more about Cameron and his mystery woman? I have a fabulous surprise for you coming! Their story will arrive in the late spring and it'll be FREE for the first few days! Sign up here to receive an alert when their book is available for a FREE download!

Also, if you're eager to dive into a my next rom-com, grab BEST LAID PLANS!! And escape into a sexy, witty, friends-to-lovers, lessons-in-seduction rom-com with a twist!

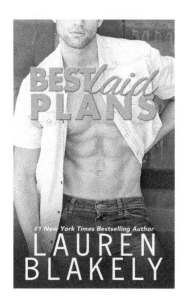

After that is ALL NIGHT LONG, a novella specially priced at release! Don't miss ALL NIGHT LONG!

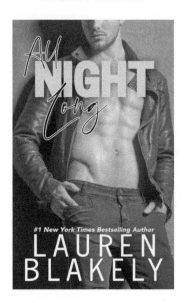

ALSO BY LAUREN BLAKELY

FULL PACKAGE, the #1 New York Times Bestselling romantic comedy!

BIG ROCK, the hit New York Times Bestselling standalone romantic comedy!

MISTER O, also a New York Times Bestselling standalone romantic comedy!

WELL HUNG, a New York Times Bestselling standalone romantic comedy!

JOY RIDE, a USA Today Bestselling standalone romantic comedy!

HARD WOOD, a USA Today Bestselling standalone romantic comedy!

THE SEXY ONE, a New York Times Bestselling bestselling standalone romance!

THE HOT ONE, a USA Today Bestselling bestselling standalone romance!

THE KNOCKED UP PLAN, a multi-week USA Today and Amazon Charts Bestselling bestselling standalone romance!

MOST VALUABLE PLAYBOY, a sexy multi-week USA Today Bestselling sports romance! And its companion sports romance, MOST LIKELY TO SCORE!

THE V CARD, a USA Today Bestselling sinfully sexy romantic comedy!

WANDERLUST, a USA Today Bestselling contemporary romance!

COME AS YOU ARE, a Wall Street Journal and multi-week USA Today Bestselling contemporary romance!

PART-TIME LOVER, a multi-week USA Today Bestselling contemporary romance!

UNBREAK MY HEART, an emotional second chance contemporary romance!

The Heartbreakers! The USA Today and WSJ Bestselling rock star series of standalone!

The New York Times and USA Today Bestselling Seductive Nights series including *Night After Night*, *After This Night*, and *One More Night*

And the two standalone romance novels in the Joy Delivered

Duet, *Nights With Him* and Forbidden Nights, both New York Times and USA Today Bestsellers!

Sweet Sinful Nights, Sinful Desire, Sinful Longing and Sinful Love, the complete New York Times Bestselling high-heat romantic suspense series that spins off from Seductive Nights!

Playing With Her Heart, a USA Today bestseller, and a sexy Seductive Nights spin-off standalone! (Davis and Jill's romance)

21 Stolen Kisses, the USA Today Bestselling forbidden new adult romance!

Caught Up In Us, a New York Times and USA Today Bestseller! (Kat and Bryan's romance!)

Pretending He's Mine, a Barnes & Noble and iBooks Bestseller! (Reeve & Sutton's romance)

Trophy Husband, a New York Times and USA Today Bestseller! (Chris & McKenna's romance)

Far Too Tempting, the USA Today Bestselling standalone romance! (Matthew and Jane's romance)

Stars in Their Eyes, an iBooks bestseller! (William and Jess' romance)

My USA Today bestselling No Regrets series that includes

The Thrill of It (Meet Harley and Trey)

and its sequel

Every Second With You

My New York Times and USA Today Bestselling Fighting Fire series that includes

Burn For Me (Smith and Jamie's romance!)

Melt for Him (Megan and Becker's romance!)

and *Consumed by You* (Travis and Cara's romance!)

The Sapphire Affair series...

The Sapphire Affair

The Sapphire Heist

Out of Bounds

A New York Times Bestselling sexy sports romance

The Only One

A second chance love story!

Stud Finder

A sexy, flirty romance!

CONTACT

I love hearing from readers! You can find me on Twitter at LaurenBlakely3, Instagram at LaurenBlakelyBooks, Facebook at LaurenBlakelyBooks, or online at LaurenBlakely.com. You can also email me at laurenblakelybooks@gmail.com

CPSIA information can be obtained
at www.ICGtesting.com
Printed in the USA
BVHW032113260319
543818BV00001B/52/P

9 781732 575523